Acknowledgments

I would like to thank my husband Randy and all of my daughters; Leslie, Laura, Lindsay and Leigha, for all of your love and positive support when I decided to pursue my dream of writing. Thank you for taking time to give me insights and feedback that improved not only the book but me, as a writer and a person.

I love you all to pieces, forever and always.

I also would like to thank Skip Coryell and White Feather Press. Without Skip's expertise and help, I would still be spinning in the quagmire of trying to figure out how to get published. I'll be forever grateful.

All i Want for Christmas is an Alibi

Linda Shoaf

Published by White Feather Press. (www.whitefeatherpress.com)

ISBN 978-1-61808-900-7

Cover design by Ron Bell

White Feather Press

Reaffirming Faith in God, Family, and Country!

Dedication

To Mom and Grams, you both inspired me to be who I am and taught me not to be afraid to dream.

CHAPTER 1

IT WAS A DARK AND STORMY NIGHT. A very dark and very stormy night. I sort of felt like the Red Baron on a mission, all alone battling the incoming onslaught. Although I'm not up against a barrage of bullets. Not gunpowder and lead, just snow beating down relentlessly. Never ending. It has been snowing for hours now. Started heavy and wet and now it has turned into the larger, light flakes that so easily blow and drift. I don't know what I was thinking heading north on a night like this. This is absolutely insane. Running away from a broken relationship to hide and heal by myself. Two days before Christmas. I truly must be insane. Seriously, no one in their right mind would dump their attractive, very successful (if that is defined as having a ridiculously high paying job) boyfriend two days before Christmas and then try and drive on a night like this. In the blizzard to beat all blizzards, in Michigan.

Insane. That pretty much sums me up. Me, Lacey Wheeler. Poster child for a woman, not in her right mind. Not sure anyone would blame me really. Five foot ten inches with a name like Lacey. I was named after an 80's TV show detective. Mom's favorite show she was binge watching while sitting awake waiting for me to quit pushing on her bladder was Cagney & Lacey. She was thankful I waited to arrive until after the final episode. In her gratitude I was named after one of the leading characters. Her favorite character was actually Cagney but mom thought people might think I was being named after James so she went with Lacey. I'm not actually very lacey, as in dainty and frilly, at all. I got my father's height and mom's smaller bone structure and angular features. I have blonde hair with a little bit of natural curl that comes from my grandma Edna. Well, at least I think that is where they came from, hers might have been from perms. If my hair was shorter and straighter, I might make a good poster child for The Rifleman. Sorta look like him. No sideburns, just big boobs. I got those from mom too.

My 35 inch inseam and 36 inch chest were a curse growing up. I'm not very good at meeting men that aren't just trying to cop a feel. Luckily, I thought I'd met the love of my life seven years ago when I met Chad Wexler. I foolishly thought my dating woes were over. He had just passed the bar exam and was working for a small firm that specializes in helping low income clients with whatever their legal needs might be. I thought I had life by the tail and it would be forever blissful. That was seven years ago when Chad and I first became a couple. Guess we have been together all of my adult formative years. We had what I thought was a happy life for five years after we met. Chad was never ready to commit but I thought I was completely ok with that. I wasn't sure I wanted to settle down anyway. Whatever settle down means.

Things started to go sideways with Chad when he quit his job and went to work for Sweeney & Todd. Better known in Grand Rapids as the premier ambulance chasers. They specialize in trumped up and outrageous lawsuits against poor undeserving people or companies. Chad loves it. I have seen a whole new side of him over the past couple years while he has ambitiously worked to get elevated to partner in the firm. I really don't like who he has turned into any more. I don't really like who I am turning into being with him anymore. It is why I am leaving. Our relationship has died on the vine and I'm dying along with it. It is time to move on.

I finally woke up and decided I'm actually able to stand on my own two feet. I just broke up with Chad at his office downtown. He works a ridiculous number of hours and never home anymore so it really was the best place to catch him. I didn't really want to do it two days before Christmas but I just could not stand it anymore. Why keep pretending? Even though things have been basically dead between us for what seems like forever, I did sort of expect him to react a little bit more than he did. He didn't even get up from his desk. Grimaced a little like he was in pain or something but basically told me I didn't know what I was talking about and that he would talk to me when he gets home. That was it. No sadness or compassion. Just telling me what to do. Well, surprise Mr. Control-freak Chad. I am not going home. Ha. What a jerk. I really should be happy. Not sure why I don't actually feel anything.

Now that I have opened my mouth and said how I feel, I can't put the words back in. I can't keep plodding along, keeping my mouth shut and faking orgasms anymore. I just can't. Besides I don't want to go back to Chad and his greed and desire to sue anyone or any company if it moves him closer to the partner office. He's definitely not the young and upcoming lawyer willing to sacrifice his time and energy to do good in the world that I fell for. There's got to be more to life.

Not that I will find it running and hiding. Pretty sure I'm never going to find it at Flight Guidance Enterprises (FGE). That's the company I work for. They make airplane avionics, software and hardware. Not always very exciting ... but sometimes. I was recently promoted out of a small 8 foot by 8 foot cube to manager of a small team. Now I have a double wide (very impressive 16 feet by 16 feet, two small cubes combined). Movin' on up. That's me. It is a good job. I work in sales so I get to work with all the departments as well as customers and I get to travel on the company dime. I've loved the flexibility and getting to see so many places around the world. Corporate America's not really glamorous or very thrilling but it pays the bills and isn't terrible most days.

I get to live vicariously through my best friend and sister LuAnn anyway. She's named after my Uncle Lou and Ann Margaret. Another favorite actress of mom's (she clearly was obsessed with oldies TV and movies). Fortunately LuAnn took after Ann in the looks department and not Uncle Lou. She's petite, strawberry blonde and well built. She's four years older than me. She's an RN and works occasionally for her heart surgeon husband Harry Hartman. He had an epiphany as a kid that his

name was a vocational omen. It has worked out well for
him. LuAnn and Harry met in college, fell completely
in love and had two sets of twins two years apart as soon
as Harry graduated. Her life exhausts me. She's settled
down enough for the both of us. Makes me not regret
having kids of my own. I am totally fine with being the
good aunt, even though my biological clock is probably
ticking. I get plenty of exposure to raising kids and settling down through her.

LuAnn hasn't had much reciprocal vicarious living
from me for quite a long time. It isn't like Chad and my
relationship just broke. It has been broken for a long,
long time. Hard to remember when it was a loving relationship. LuAnn has noticed and complained recently
that my free spirit seems to have died and she isn't able
to live vicariously through my life. She loved that I'd
always enjoyed a very different life from her own. I
travel for work and Chad and I were always escaping to
some exotic location or another. And we used to have a
healthy sex life. Not that I gave her all the gory details
but I would share some. Not anything of a bodily nature,
just stuff like some of the unique locations Chad and I
would get carried away in---an elevator, the hill beside the
football stadium, the golf course, that kind of thing. She
would get a kick out of my sense of adventure. Honestly,
I can't remember anymore the last time Chad and I made
love anywhere. Chad has been too busy building his career. We never see each other when we have any energy
or to even touch enough to have any sparks.

So, I just broke up with him and now I am moving on.
Not an option to stick around right now. Grand Rapids
is a good-sized city but really a small town at heart.   A

pretty nice place to live. Big enough yet small enough that you can get anywhere in the entire metro area in less than thirty minutes. Well on most days. Not snowy days like this one. There is quite a bit to do in GR and it is a great place to raise a family (if you can get a guy to commit) and not so bad for singles either. It is "Beer City USA" if you like beer, that is handy. GR is also close enough to bigger cities like Chicago and Detroit that it is easy to get the big city fix when you want it. Maybe the most attractive feature of Grand Rapids is its proximity to the big lake. Lake Michigan. It is awesome. Like the ocean but no salt. Or sharks. Love it most of the time. Except on days like today. If this is lake-effect snow, it can stop any time now.

As soon as word gets out I broke up with The Chad Wexler, rising star on the fast track for partner at Sweeney & Todd, biggest law firm in town, my phone will ring off the hook as they say. Already turned it off. Just in case he calls begging me to come back. Not that I honestly expect that to happen. No one will believe I left him vs the other way around. Pretty sure there is a betting pool in his office on how long he would stay with me. They'll place a bet on anything. They are all a bunch of intelligent, but essentially dumb rich kids who have no integrity whatsoever so I really don't care what they think, but I really don't want to face anyone yet. I would rather just hide.

Which is exactly why it is off to the north I go. LuAnn has a cottage on a small lake about an hour north of town. I use the word cottage loosely because it is bigger than most homes. Harry does well in his chosen trade. He is the best heart surgeon in town, maybe the country. Sadly there is a lot of demand for his talent. Though, I'm thankful I have a rich sister that I can mooch off of. We were going to spend Christmas together up here anyway. I'm just going a day early. I guess I should call her and let her know what I have done. I am just going to take some extra time at her lake house to get my act together before the family shows up and starts hammering me with questions. I'll have to wait to call her until after I get there, if I ever do get there on these roads. I can turn my phone back on and charge it then. It is basically outta juice and once we get talking it can take a while to get off the phone. Plus, no way I can dial, talk and then drive in this weather.

These roads are absolutely ridiculous. The slush and snow is so thick it's grabbing at the tires and taking most of my strength to stay in the two track that is supposedly 131 North. It's like the wheels have a mind of their own. It's impossible to see more than two feet in front of Hank (my beloved 4Runner, Hank the Tank). If I happen to drive up on anyone else insane enough to be out here, they are inching along slower than I am and it is even more impossible to pass. I swear, if I could be made queen for a day I really would "fix the damn roads". That's the annoying and slightly offensive slogan the last governor used to ride into office. Surprise, no real progress yet. If it were me, I would get them enough plows to keep up with these friggin' Michigan winters and I would make some new road rules. First one would be starting November 1st through March 1st the left lane would be designated for the slow lane and the right lane the passing lane. Just the opposite of what we do now. The right lane is the only one they consistently try to keep clear and if you are just going to putz along like you learned to drive in Georgia then you can stick to the slow lane on the left. Makes perfect sense. Can't believe they haven't thought of it by now. It would be better and safer for everybody.

Well, maybe not the putzing Georgia drivers but for true Michiganders it would be perfect.

I really just want to be able to get out of here faster. Not that I could actually drive faster than 20 miles an hour right now but it is the principle. On the bright side, the monster truck in front of me is at least making a path through these drifts even if it is slow going. At this rate, the usual just over an hour drive is going to take at least three hours. Hopefully not four. Not sure I can maintain my death grip on the wheel that long. I will feel so much better once I can get out of this car.

Seems odd we've ended up being the only two vehicles on the entire freeway. Not that I can see very far. Maybe there is more traffic out here than it seems. Feels like we are the only two on the face of the earth right now. Eerie kind of. Maybe if I turn on the radio I won't feel so disconnected from the real world.

Who says God doesn't have a sense of humor. First thing I hear when I turn on the radio is Rodney Atkins belting out the chorus to "If you are going through hell". 'Things go from bad to worse and you keep on going, don't slow down'. Country music, so appropriate and good advice in real-life situations. Was God telling me to just keep on going? I was thinking of maybe turning around and begging Chad to take me back. Could I really lie and tell him I didn't mean anything I said? Probably not. Though it might be worth it to get my Christmas present. I'm pretty sure the Louboutins I saw peeking out from under his desk were meant for me. They are probably knock offs since they weren't in a box but they looked adorable and perfect for me. He probably picked them up on some side street in China when he went for those client meetings last month. He would never, ever buy me a pair at full price. For himself definitely. Me, not in a million years. They probably are not worth going back for. Definitely not worth losing what remaining shred of dignity I still have.

Breaking news on the radio, I had better focus. The 131 freeway is closed. Really? What about me and the monster truck out here? I've never, ever known them to close the freeway. I know it is bad out but not so bad they would actually close the freeway. I thought it was just me panicking, thinking things are worse than they really are. Didn't realize this storm has created a statewide emergency. They haven't seen anything this bad since the storm of 1978. This might be worse. The snow had started out thick and wet, the kind that grabs car tires forcing the drivers to hold the driving wheel tightly in the 10 and 2 position. Failure to remain vigilant would find the distracted driver deep in the ditch. The storm switched over to lighter, blowing snow. Coming down with a vengeance. Five to ten foot drifts expected. People should be prepared to be snowed in for days. Merry Christmas everybody. Sucks if you are a procrastinator and left any shopping for last minute. Thankfully I am prepared. We were planning on going up to LuAnn's anyway so I had to get everything done early. Now I just had to make it there alive and hope they clear the roads in a day instead of days. Christmas will be here soon. Glad I am getting off this freeway even sooner. At least I hope I am. I think that was the Howard City exit I just passed a little bit ago. Gets so dark up here and with all this snow, it is hard to tell.

What luck, the monster truck is taking the same exit I am. Maybe he will make me a path all the way to the lake. Crap, no such luck. Looks like he is turning left and headed towards Hardy Dam. No one was heading right with me. No one was heading anywhere here. Snow deeper and drifting more too. It's worse on the north/south roads, glad I mostly just have to head east, and don't have much farther north to go. Hold on Hank, not too much further.

Linda Shoaf

CHAPTER 2

SAFE AT LAST. HOW I MANAGED to get pulled into LuAnn's garage, I'll never know. So glad she let me program her spare stall door to Hank the Tank. I pulled in and slowly peeled my hands from the steering wheel. I just sat there for a few minutes catching my breath. Nothing has been plowed from the highway to here. A very slow going 10 miles. It might take them days to clear the roads.

I paused as I went into the house. I always love coming up here. LuAnn has done a fantastic job of making the perfect cozy cabin. It definitely wasn't small but she was an expert at making it feel cozy. I stepped into the living room and was surprised to see the tree lights on. It brought tears to my eyes as I remembered it was Christmas after all. The tree was only an eight footer, not quite as magnificent as the twelve foot one she had at the house in GR but it was beautifully done with rustic and cabin type ornaments and just the right amount of soft white lights. I could swear I even picked up a faint scent of pine.

I didn't bother turning any other lights on. I could find my way up the stairs by the light from the tree. As soon as I got to my room (the spare bedroom I always use when I am up here), I hear LuAnn yelling my name over the intercom asking me what I am doing. What? She is already up here? Where is she? So weird, I didn't notice any other vehicles in the other garage stalls. Was I that out of it when I dragged myself in here? I shook my head, amazed I could even drive and thankful Hank came through for me as if on autopilot.

I crept through the dark house, afraid to turn on any more lights until I figured out what's going on. Suddenly, the living room lights came on and LuAnn yelled for me to get over to the communication console in the office so she could talk to me. Seriously like the Jetsons or something around here. I forgot about all the gadgets they have for monitoring the house and controlling the lights and temperature. At the communication center we could even have a video chat back with the home base. All the comforts of a cozy northland cottage, for spoiled brats.

"What are you doing walking around the house in the dark for Pete's sake? Why haven't you answered any of my calls or texts? I have been trying to get hold of you for over an hour!"

I jumped out of my skin a little bit, "LuAnn, for shit sake. You scared the crap out of me. I just got here at the lake. It is awful out. I didn't turn on the lights because I could see well enough by the lights on the tree, which you left on by the way. And do you know your fake tree smells faintly like pine? I haven't seen any text or got your calls because I was preoccupied driving on very treacherous roads. If you haven't noticed there is a blizzard out there. I was going to call and explain that I was on my way up here but my phone was nearly dead and I turned it off. I need to get it turned back on." I started digging through my purse that I had dropped on the stairs to try and find it.

LuAnn started screaming at me, "For God sake, DO NOT turn on your phone!" Then she calmly added, "And the tree lights are on a timer, along with the essential oil diffuser for the homy smell. Do you like it?" I swear she is slightly schizophrenic.

I rolled my eyes but was curious, "yes I do like the smell but how in the world do you keep water in it if you are not here?"

LuAnn huffed, "Do not roll your eyes at me. It is a design kinda like a coffee machine with a water reservoir. Works great. You should get one."

I forgot she could see my every move. I'd have to remember to be more careful. But wait, "what are you talking about? I get the timer and diffuser technology but why on earth would I leave my phone off? Are you nuts?"

"Oh, right, well, the police are looking for you. Chad's been murdered and they seem to think you did it. I'm just thankful I was home by the house monitoring system and heard it ping when you pulled into the garage. I watched you sit there for at least five minutes and thought something was really wrong with you. I couldn't get you to hear me with your earmuffs on. Which you look ridiculous in by the way."

I just shook my head, surely, I didn't hear her correctly. Chad could not have been murdered. No way. She would not idly tell me about her high tech tree aroma and combine that in a sentence where she is critiquing my fashion sense without leading with something like I was wanted for murder. Would she? "LuAnn, that is crazy talk. I just broke up with Chad. That is it. And these earmuffs are cute and look perfect on me. What are you talking about?"

"Listen honey. Trust me, you look ridiculous. The police were just here. They showed me pictures of the crime scene. Chad is definitely dead."

I couldn't stop shaking my head and was starting to shake all over. "No way LuAnn. That's impossible. Chad was fine when I left his office and I came straight here. It did take nearly three hours but he was totally fine when I left him. Well, hopefully he wasn't really totally fine. I was hoping he's more heartbroken than he was letting on but I am sure he was still breathing and somewhat seething when I last saw him." I paused, closing my eyes to think and catch my breath. I slowly continued, "technically, Chad didn't actually even seeth that much come to think of it. I told him I did not want to see him anymore and he didn't even get up out of his chair, or step away from his desk to come and stop me or comfort me or anything. He seemed almost stunned and glued to his chair. He's probably still sitting there working away. There is no way he was murdered. They must have the wrong guy. I'm sure he is probably still in his office working late."

It was LuAnn's turn to shake her head. "Well, the police were just here and not too happy to have to be out in this weather. When I couldn't tell them where you were, they tried scaring me into confessing and showed me a picture of the crime scene and I'm telling you, he is in his office alright and definitely not moving on his own volition because there is a huge pair of scissors right in his heart."

Being a nurse and not so faint of heart, LuAnn could take seeing something like that. I dropped to the floor at the thought. Thankfully I missed hitting anything vital when I went down and LuAnn was patient enough to wait for me to process it all.

"LuAnn, there is no way it could have been him. I just saw him a little over three hours ago. And there is absolutely, positively, no way they can even remotely think I did it. They just need to talk to Sara Jones, Chad's administrative assistant. She can vouch for me. She was there working right outside his office when I got there and I left the door open once I went in so I am sure she heard every word we said. I even almost went back in. I turned around at the elevator and went back but his door was closed again. It sounded like he was on a call. Sara was still there and told me how proud she was of me and that she had always admired me. She told me it must have been hard but I did the right thing and that he didn't deserve me. I'm sure she will tell all of that to the police. They just need to talk to her."

"Well Lacey, they can't yet. She was attacked too. She's alive but just barely. If she hangs on, maybe it will get cleared up. But that is a big if. If she doesn't make it, you are going to be wanted for both murders. I am trying to keep close tabs on her at the hospital. It is touch and go right now. They have put her into a medically induced coma to help her body rest and heal. I have asked for the best staff to care for her and know they will keep me advised if her condition changes at all. If she makes it through the next 48 hours, she might recover. Let's pray that she does."

I was still sitting on the floor shaking my head. "I really can't believe this is happening right now. Who would have murdered Chad and attacked Sara? She was so sweet, and, ok, Chad might have been a jerk 99% of the time but not annoying enough to be murdered? It is so mind boggling. I just cannot believe it. I wanted to be rid of him but I didn't want him dead. What in the world am I going to do?"

LuAnn put her hands on her hips and had her big-sister panties on I could tell. She told me to get off the floor and get hold of myself. "There's nothing you can do at the moment. It's really a good thing you didn't go home or you would be spending Christmas in the slammer. Just lay low and do not turn on your phone. I am going to turn off the inside cameras and intercom so you don't have to get weird about me watching and listening to you. It would be weird and I really don't want the kids stumbling in here and seeing you walking around the house and wondering what is going on. You will hear the system beep if I turn anything on to talk to you. I just had the house cleaned and groceries delivered when I was getting ready for us to be up there for the holidays so you should have plenty to eat and be comfortable. Right now we are really uncertain when it will be safe enough to travel and we will be able to get up there. They have called in the National Guard to help stranded people and to help deal with clearing the roads. The police even gave Harry a ride back to the hospital in their Hummer-type vehicle so he could stay there in case he is needed for any heart emergencies. Just try to get some sleep and we can talk about next steps tomorrow."

Easy for her to say.

Linda Shoaf

CHAPTER 3

AFTER A BASICALLY SLEEPLESS night, I awoke to one of those dazzling winter days that almost takes your breath away. The sun shining off the white snow crystals was blinding. Michigan can be weird like that. Stormy one minute, sunny the next. The sun always makes everything seem better. Typically the view across the lake was sparkling water and lots of tall white pines. Today, the snow had obliterated almost everything. Looking out across the lake, it looked like one huge mass of white. With the frigid weather we had earlier this month, the lake had already frozen over and was snow covered. I could barely make out other homes around the lake. There were only about a dozen people that lived here year round. Most of the cottages were built for summer only. People came up in May to open them and then they boarded them back up in September or October. They were short seasoners and it didn't look like many, if any, had made it up for the holidays. A few, like LuAnn and Harry, kept the place open year-round but only made it up occasionally in the winter. For the holidays or maybe a weekend of ice fishing.

Absolutely crazy how much snow there is out there. It had blown and drifted so much you couldn't even see where I pulled into the drive and garage. Not sure how I will be able to back out of there until they clear the roads anyway. Which is fine by me. I might enjoy having the place to myself for a few days.

I spent Christmas Eve, laying in the sun coming in through the huge front windows in the living room. If I closed my eyes real tight, I could almost pretend I was on a beach far, far away with a beautiful Christmas tree as my palm tree. Last night had to have been just a really horrible dream. The breakup, the drive and then discovering Chad had been brutally murdered in his office. Unbelievable. I mean, sure, I'd wanted to slap the smug look off his face when I walked into his office yesterday but I wouldn't have killed him. Even if the thought may have crossed my mind. The way he just bit his lip like he was trying to hold back a laugh or something and then just stared at me when I told him we were through. In his typical condescending way he had told me I was being too rash and he gave his orders that we would talk about it later when he got home. I told him I had taken all my things and moved out and I wouldn't be there. He acted strange but then I'm not sure what I really expected. I'd never broken up with anyone like this before. I thought he might at least get up and come hug me or kiss me. Slap me maybe. Anything. Nope. He just sat there with the weird, pained look on his face. He might have moaned. So weird. Maybe I had hurt him. Hard to tell. He was almost like a statue stuck in his chair. Though he did jerk once and shuffle his feet because that is when I noticed the

Louboutin shoes. They moved like he had bumped them. So strange. Why he would leave my cheap out of the box knockoff present under his desk is beyond me.

And why would anyone attack Sara? Maybe she had walked in and surprised the killer and tried to fight him off or something. She must have been away from her desk when the killer went in because he would have had to walk right past her to get into Chad's office. She was working on cutting out pictures for a storyboard Chad was working on. Maybe she needed supplies from the stock-room or went to the restroom or something. Oh my God. The scissors the killer used must have been the ones Sara was using! She probably left them laying on top of her desk when she walked away. My mind was a complete jumble of thoughts. I couldn't stop my mind from churning, wondering just what had happened after I left Chad's office last night.

My semi-bliss in the sun was suddenly interrupted by a loud knock at the door. I think I jumped six feet in the air before running to hide. I was scared to death the cops were on to me. Though how they would have gotten through all this snow was a mystery. I got my heart out of my throat and went to try and peek out the side window. Thankful again for my spoiled sister and her high tech home with tinted windows no one could see in through, I figured I was safe if I didn't move much. I couldn't help but gasp out loud. I froze and tried to still my racing heart. I was looking into the most beautiful blue eyes I had ever seen. They looked just like the Caribbean sea I had just been imagining I was sunning by. They were evenly spaced in the face of a Grecian god. With face stubble.

The handsome lumberjack that belonged to those eyes

and that sexy stubble was talking to a shorter, older, silver version of himself, minus the stubble and incredible body. Mr. Handsome had sunglasses raised up on his head and was trying to look through the windows tinted glass. I missed most of their conversation but I think they were checking if anyone was home because the silver fox thought he had seen lights last night. They walked away so I assumed the incredible hunk must have convinced him he was wrong. No one here. Whew that was close.

I watched them cross back through the tracks they had just made through the waist-high snow. They went back towards the house on the right. It was large like LuAnn's house but was older. Owned by a family that had handed the cottage down for generations. Oh, I remember the silver fox now. Mr. Palmer. I hadn't seen Murray in a long time. He seems to have aged really well. I don't remember the hunkalicious guy with him though. Don't remember any of Murray's grandkids looking quite that good. I'll have to ask LuAnn whenever she hollers at me again. Which reminds me she is due any moment now.

Within minutes I could hear the ding of the intercom and LuAnn calling my name. Funny how that often happens, have a thought and the same thing happens. Like cosmically connected or something. LuAnn sounded like I felt, completely out of sorts.

I was hammering her with questions before she could even get a word out. "What is going on? Have you heard any news on Sara? Can they wake her up yet? What took you so long to call?" Before she could answer, I heard her doorbell and she put me on hold and muted my end. How rude. Pretty sure I am the most important and pressing issue she has at the moment.

I could hear a man who identified himself as Detective

Rodriquez asking her if she had any information on my whereabouts that she cared to share with him. Ok, maybe the detective at the door trumps my importance. LuAnn being the terrific sister she is, lied smoothly and told him no. I realized then that I was still staring into the camera and that if the Rodriquez looked into the communication room he would see me sitting here live and in person. Crap. I ducked under the desk so I couldn't be seen but could still listen in.

His questioning was pretty lame. He just wanted to know what she knew about Chad and our relationship and if she knew why I had taken all of my belongings out of the house we shared. They were thinking I had planned Chad's murder and they wanted to stress how much more serious the charge was for premeditated murder. They had the video surveillance footage from the office building where Chad's office was located. The cameras covered the parking levels, in the elevators and the area near the elevator doors on each floor. They knew I had parked illegally on the employees only level of the parking garage. He said they saw me park next to Chad's car and then stop and stare at some other vehicle in the garage. They also saw me walk to the elevator and access the employee only floor for Chad's office . They also knew that I had gone towards Chad's office and 15 minutes later was back at the elevator but paused and turned back towards his office only to return to the elevator 10 minutes later. Wondered if LuAnn had any possible explanation for my actions on those tapes.

LuAnn could honestly tell them she had no idea why I had taken everything since I hadn't had a chance to completely fill her in on my drastic decision. She also told them she knew Chad and I had been drifting apart but didn't realize I had reached the decision to leave him. She stressed that she did know me well enough to know I would never harm anyone let alone murder them. She urged them to broaden their investigation since a killer was obviously still on the loose.

He didn't seem moved by her plea but didn't seem to be able to come up with any more questions for her at the moment. He gave her his card and told her to call if she heard from me.

I could hear LuAnn come back into the communication room and take me off mute. Then she let me have it in the way only older sisters can. "I am not going to keep lying for you! I'm pretty sure they were suspicious but thankfully it is Christmas Eve and they didn't seem to want to keep grilling me with questions about my derelict sister. I'm sweating bullets over here as an accessory to aiding and abetting a suspected murderer. I'm pretty sure that is a felony. I love you but I am not going in the slammer for you!"

"Geese Louise Lu, you are such a drama queen. Calm down." I say this as I am sweating bullets myself and still shaking from my two back to back near misses of being discovered. I took a couple of deep breaths to release some of the tension and tried again. "I'm sorry for being so agitated and peppering you with questions before you even get a chance to say hello. First thing I really wanted to find out is what you have heard about Sara. Is she ok?"

"She made it through the night but it is still touch and go. They are keeping her in the ICU and she is in very serious condition. They won't be able to talk to her until they can bring her out of the coma and even then it might not be right away. It could take awhile. Another thing to consider is that the attack might have been so traumatic for her she might have trouble remembering much of what happened that day. She may not be your best defense in keeping you out of the slammer."

"Would you quit saying that! No one is going to the slammer! I did not do anything wrong. Well, if you don't count me not stopping to get my Christmas present from Chad before I broke up with him. That really was my only mistake. I did not do anything more to him than hurt his feelings and by the way he acted, that was marginal."

"Really Lacey? You think your only mistake was not grabbing a Christmas present! You break up with him after working hours at his office so there are basically no witnesses and they can see you going back and forth to his office. What the hell were you thinking?!!"

"Hey, hey, hey. There were Louboutins under his desk that were my Christmas present. It didn't dawn on me until I was driving up here that I should have taken them. And before you say anything, yes Mr. Cheapskate got knockoffs for me. Remember when he went to China last month. He must have picked them up then. They weren't in a box but they looked real and definitely cute. I should have grabbed them. Granted I get it, I didn't make the best choices. If only Sara could wake up and tell them. I am sure she heard every word we said. She didn't actually look up when I left his office. Like she was embarrassed to have eavesdropped on our private conversation. I didn't blame her, I was embarrassed myself. I turned around at the elevator because I was thinking about going back and apologizing and caving in. Sara seemed relieved I didn't try to barge back in his office and she seemed genuine in her praise of me. The only reason it took me longer to get back to the elevator was that I went to the restroom to clean up my face. I had been crying and I was a big hot mess. I had mascara all over. Once I had composed myself, I left. Unfortunately, I didn't see or run into anyone else the short time I was there. I wish I had some way to figure out who killed Chad. I'm not sure what to do since I am stuck up here."

LuAnn tried to console me, "The shoes probably smelled like toxic plastic the way a lot of the really cheap products from China do. You would have hated them. You did the right thing leaving them there. Just sit tight and we will think of something to get you out of this mess. At least no one should be able to find you for a while."

"That reminds me, a couple of men came to the door just before you rang me up. They about scared me to death. I thought they had found me out and were here to drag me away. I didn't recognize either of them at first but then I remembered Mr. Palmer owned the place next door. The younger one with him was a mouth-watering hunk. I figure he must be a grandson because he looked similar but much younger and a whole lot hunkier. Did you know he had such a handsome grandson?"

LuAnn got a Cheshire cat-like grin, "Oh, that would be Luke. Stop drooling. You remember him don't you? Sheila Jackson's brother. Maybe you haven't been up when he has been around. Their father was Murray and Shirley's son, Mike. Murray has been a widower for at least ten years now so you probably don't remember his wife Shirley. I forgot Sheila told me they would all be up there for the holidays too. Luke is a state trooper and a really nice guy. Why would he and Murray be coming over to the house?"

"Apparently Murray thought he saw lights last night. He must have seen me as I pulled into the garage. Luke is absolutely gorgeous. I only peeked at him through the side window but even under all the snow gear he looked very tall and extremely well built and he has the best blue eyes ever."

LuAnn jumped out of her chair, doing a victory dance like I'd made a touchdown, "Oh my gosh, Lacey, that's it! I've got a solution! Well, not to everything but Sheila's husband is Hunter Jackson. You know, probably the best lawyer in town. You need a good attorney. I will get hold of Sheila and see if they made it up there before the storm hit. If Hunter's there, you can meet him and give him your side of the story before the cops nab you!"

"Would you flippin' stop that for crying out loud! The cops are not going to nab me. I do like the idea of getting the best lawyer in town but not sure I can actually afford him."

LuAnn plopped back into her chair, "What are you saying? You can't not afford him. You do look good in orange but I'm not so sure you are prison material. Have you seen Orange is the New Black? And jumpsuits, definitely not you. Nevermind. Let me call Sheila and I'll call, well, intercom you right back."

With that she hung up on me. My head was spinning. Maybe I'd just go back and try and find my happy place in the sun. The sun looked like it was starting to fade quickly over the lake. It gets dark so early this time of year. I would be plunged into darkness soon. I had better go and close all the blinds in my room so I could barricade myself in for the night. I didn't want to risk anyone seeing any glimmer of light through the tinting and ratting myself out.

Before I could even get to the stairs, LuAnn was pinging me back. She had good news and bad news. Great news that Hunter agreed to represent me and as a bonus, for half his usual fee. Bad news, he did not make it up north before the storm hit. Sheila and their two kids, Luke and their parents, Mike and Joan, were already up here with Murrary along with the family dog, Bruce. They had come up earlier this week while Hunter was stuck wrapping up a case in GR. Now Hunter would be home alone for Christmas.

LuAnn started to caution me not to despair. "Before you get your panties in a twist, Hunter had a great suggestion that will help you, as well as get Harry and me off the hook for harboring a fugitive. He wants you to turn yourself in."

I bent down in my chair and hung my head between my knees feeling totally defeated. "Just how in the world am I supposed to do that? I can't go anywhere."

Lu remained calm, "Hunter is going to arrange for you to turn yourself in to Luke. Then you will stay under house arrest until the roads are cleared and Luke can transport you back to GR. You will be in Luke's custody. Harry is so relieved we aren't going to be in trouble for harboring a fugitive either. You're back in his good graces. It's a great solution for both of us."

Now it was my turn to jump out of my chair, just not with joy. "Wait, what?!! Have Mr. Gorgeous apprehend me? Isn't there some other option? That is not exactly how I wanted to meet him. Poop on a stick. That would be awful. There has got to be a better alternative." I felt frantic and could feel the panic rise in me.

LuAnn remained steadfast in her nurse-steady calm. "There's not. Relax. It will be fine. Luke will come over later tomorrow night. You can have a peaceful Christmas. I am sure you and Luke can work out a decent arrangement until they get the roads cleared. Should only be a couple more days. It's not like you have to wear hand-cuffs or anything. Unless you are into that sort of thing." She snorted when she laughed, "just kidding. Really, it will work out great. Hunter wants to have a video call before Luke takes you into custody so to speak so we will call you tomorrow night. Merry Christmas."

With that, she hung up on me again. I stuck my tongue out at the screen only to realize she had just cut me off from seeing her. I heard her say, 'I saw that' before fully disconnecting the call. Perfect. Big sister eyes and ears 24/7. And I get to look forward to humiliating myself on Christmas with a 6'5" tower of tight muscles with eyes I could swim in.

What else could go wrong?

CHAPTER 4

I DECIDED TO PACE THE LIVING ROOM in the dark before confining myself to my room. I felt shut off from the world enough already. My room was a nice corner room but it didn't have the cathedral ceiling and open feeling of the living room. The living room windows that covered the wall facing the lake helped with the wide open feel too. It was a beautiful view. The sky had a few lingering streaks of pink, orange and yellow though the sun was hidden below the trees. So beautiful and serene. I wished I could hang on to this moment to keep me calm in the days ahead.

Just as I sighed and was ready to move away from the window, I saw a quick flash of light across the lake. I froze until I remembered no one could see me. What was that? Who could be out there and what could they be doing? I picked up the binoculars they had on the shelf for bird watching but it was getting too dark to make out much. About all I could tell was that Charlie Hooper was walking around his cottage. Hard to imagine what he would be up to on such a snowy, cold winter night. Charlie is the crazy old man across the lake from

LuAnn's place. Not really straight across but right in line with watching the sunset. I met him once when Lu and I were out walking. He was on a scooter and came to a screeching halt next to us. He practically screamed at us wanting to know what we thought we were doing. He had on camouflage gear and one of those ancient leather football helmets with goggles. Seriously crazy. He looked almost cross eyed and had some issue with his lips. He reminded me of Carl from Caddyshack. Only crazier. A complete nut job. LuAnn had stiffened up but put on her fake happy face and told him we were just enjoying the mild evening and walking home. He had ranted on and on that we had better not be spying on him and that we had better get home if we knew what was good for us. He puttered off as quickly as he had stopped. I avoided that side of the lake after that. No sense tempting fate or weirdos. I just hoped he would keep his craziness to himself and over there.

I grabbed Lu's Kindle and headed to bed. Pretty sad and lonely Christmas Eve. Not what I had been expecting less than 24 hours ago. Amazing how things can change so quickly. At least I wasn't curling up on a stainless steel bunk in the hoosegow with nothing to read.

My room was on the left front corner of the house. I didn't have a view of the Palmer house but from the window facing the lake, I could see across the lake to Charlie's place. From the side window I could see Mrs. Peabody's quaint little place. Gladys' home is the oldest cottage on the lake. She is another year-rounder. I glanced over her way and noticed she hadn't turned in for the night yet. All of her curtains were still open and I could see through the entire cottage. It was full of deer heads and other stuffed animals. Her late husband Elmer used to love taxidermy.

He had been gone at least a couple years but it looked like Gladys hadn't parted with any of his handiwork. She's probably as crazy as Charlie but at least she was a nice old lady with kind eyes and beautiful silver hair. Eccentric crazy not truly looney. I could see her using a huge pair of binoculars and peering out across the lake. Maybe she was wondering what Charlie was up to as well.

I read for a few hours and it helped distract my mind but as soon as I turned the Kindle off, my mind started racing again. I wish I could have fallen asleep with visions of sugar plums dancing through my head. Instead I tossed and turned with visions of Chad running from someone and Charlie's crazy scary eyes and Gladys looking at me through her huge binoculars looking a bit like Mr. Magoo. I finally gave up and got up around 4 a.m. I decided to go down and watch It's a Wonderful Life on LuAnn's awesome 70 inch TV and have popcorn for breakfast. It would be just like being at the movies. Merry Christmas to me.

I turned off the movie thinking maybe that hadn't been the best film choice. I usually love it but think it might have made me even more depressed. I definitely was not feeling like I was living "A Wonderful Life" and I know for a fact I haven't positively touched as many lives as George Bailey did and I don't even have much of a life insurance policy. I didn't need to spend Christmas feeling even more sorry for myself. I do love Clarence though. I wish I had a guardian angel to help me see my way out of the mess I had gotten myself into.

I jumped up as the doorbell started ringing and someone started banging on the door around 8 a.m. Who on earth could that be? LuAnn said I didn't have to turn myself over to Luke until tonight. I peeked out the window only to see Gladys Peabody bouncing on her feet in a parka three sizes too big for her five foot frame. She had boots that went up past her knees and she kept stomping them in an effort to keep warm. Now what should I do? Ignore her and pretend I'm not in here and let her freeze out there? Invite her in and act like it is perfectly natural that I'd be here alone on Christmas with butter stains on my pajamas?

Gladys knocked on the door again and shouted, "open up, Lacey. I know you are in there."

I slowly opened the door and she barged right in. "No sense both of us sitting alone on Christmas. Figured we could watch movies and play Scrabble. Looks like you have already beat me to part of the fun and excitement", she said as she looked me over, obviously noticing the popcorn remnants and butter stains on my pajama ensemble.

Before I could say a word she pushed past me clutching a small suitcase and a Scrabble game. "I figured you might be here. I saw you on the news and I just knew there is no way anyone as nice as you could murder anyone. Even if he was a jerk and most likely had it coming. You wouldn't do it. You didn't do it, did you?"

I could only dumbly mumble, "well, no", while shaking my head. Was she my Clarence? How did she know I was here? I no sooner had the thought and she was telling me.

"I woke up last night just after midnight. I was tossing and turning after watching Charlie for so darn long. That crazy old coot is up to something; I am sure of it. Anyway, I got up to get some warm milk to settle my nerves and as I glanced over here, it just dawned on me that of course you would be here. You and LuAnn were always very close and it is the perfect place for you to hide from the cops and all the media attention. It's all over the news how they are stumped and continuing to broaden their manhunt as the roads slowly get cleared. We've got to somehow figure out who done it before they can make their way up here. Don't you think that is a good idea?" She asked me like she was asking me over for tea.

Again, I could only mumble a positive response while nodding my head in agreement. I had the overwhelming sense I was about to be taken over by a mini-whirlwind.

Gladys shook out of her parka and practically jumped out of her boots. She looked a little elf-like in a striped pair of long johns and thick wooly socks. "I brought over a change of clothes so we could get dressed later for dinner. It's fine to be a sloth most of the day but we should spiff up a little bit for dinner." She pulled a small box out of the pocket of her parka and handed it to me. "It's not much but I didn't want to come empty handed on Christmas. Didn't want you thinking I am a complete oaf."

I snapped out of my stupor. "Really you shouldn't have. I don't have anything for you. No, wait. I do have something." I led her to the family room and snagged a small box that I had intended to give LuAnn from under the tree. "She will never miss it and it is perfect for you."

We opened our gifts and we were both genuinely grateful. For the gifts and each other's company on this beautiful, blessed day. I'd given Gladys a winter scarf that a friend had made with the softest cashmere yarn. It brought out the blue in Gladys' eyes and I think there was a bit more sparkle in them when she proudly put it on. My gift was a beautiful necklace. A mother-of-pearl carved pendant on a beautiful gold chain. It was far too generous. I started to protest but she quickly told me to hush. "It is an old one I had, just collecting dust in the jewelry box. Elmer bought it for me when we went to Hawaii. It's an antique gambling chip. I've always thought it was a bit of a good luck charm. I'm thinking if there's anybody that needs some good luck right about now it would be you, so you should have it."

She almost made me cry. She hugged me and said "we need to cheer up. Let's see if LuAnn has any good spirits to drink. I think we could both use a cup of Christmas cheer to help us get through the day."

"Thank you Mrs. Peabody. I sincerely appreciate the gift and your stopping in today. Cannot tell you how much both mean to me."

"First, you are welcome, I'm happy to help. Second, you need to call me Gladys. All my friends do. Or Glad if you want to. I answer to both. Mrs. Peabody makes me think of Elmer's mother, God rest her soul. She was old. I'm getting there but not ready to throw the towel in yet. Now, start from the beginning and tell me why the police would think you murdered that lawyer fellow and how you wound up here."

I told her I would fill her in while I made us a more proper breakfast of eggs and bacon and mimosas, heavy on the champagne. She thought that sounded wonderful and followed me into the kitchen. She jumped up on one of the counter stools and watched while I cooked. She was a spry little thing. She started to fill me in on her life and ask me about mine. "It's been awhile since I have seen you up here Lacey. What have you been up to besides this whole murder thing? Well, I know you didn't murder him but sure sounds like you need an alibi. What has been going on in your life? Mine is just sameo-sameo. You remember I lost my Earl a little over two years ago right? Now I just hang by myself mostly. Other than feeding my birds I don't get out much. I still do yoga and go to bingo night with Violet regularly I guess. It keeps me limber and in shape. You remember Violet Smith don't you? She has been my friend forever. Since grade school when she moved here in the first grade. So that is pretty close to forever. So tell me, what are you up to? How did you end up here in this weather?"

I served up our feast right on the counter and filled her in on my career at FGE and my work with the Big Sister program. Not a thrill a minute lifestyle. Then I started to explain how I got up here. First, I had to explain to her that I had decided to leave Chad for good and had spent the afternoon loading Hank the Tank with all my worldly possessions. She seemed to instinctively know that Hank was my 4Runner. I'd have to remember to ask her if she had a name for the little blue Chevette that she drove this past summer when I saw her last. I could tell she was biting her tongue on saying anything about Chad. She had him pegged as a jerk just from meeting him once here at the lake a couple years ago. Right after he had started at Sweeney & Todd. As I recall he was very cocky and looked down his nose at everyone here. Gladys had been invited to one of LuAnn's cookouts and I knew then she was not impressed with him.

As I tidied the kitchen back up, I refilled our mimosas and told her to hop down off the stool and to get comfy in the living room so I could continue to fill her in.

CHAPTER 5

GLADYS PEPPERED ME WITH questions all the way to the living room. She grilled me for details about his office, who I saw, what I noticed while I was there, what my impressions were. She kept pressing me to give her all the details of Chad's fateful night. I closed my eyes and tried to go back to that night. Was it really just two nights ago? I shook my head to clear it and started, "I had to drive slowly through the increasingly bad weather to get downtown. It seems like it took forever and I hated being out on the roads but I was determined to get the breakup over with. I parked in the firm's lower level parking garage reserved for employees only. Chad had given me the access code when he was first hired. So impressed with himself that he had free parking and was able to be so magnanimous to share it with me. It was very handy to just park there if we met downtown for anything. I had no idea it was considered illegal until the detective mentioned it. I had parked in an open slot next to Chad's BMW."

I got very still and could feel myself transporting myself back to the cold dark parking garage that seemed almost scary that night. "The lot was mostly empty. I recognized a few of the cars parked in that area. I saw Sara Jones's Santa Fe. Sara was Chad's administrative assistant. She is from Australia and has an accent. She's a nice woman who is a bodybuilder as a hobby. She doesn't deserve having to work for Chad. He was a bit of a workaholic and expected the same out of her. I wasn't surprised to see that she was there.

I also recognized Gary Smith's Yukon. Gary is another attorney that started about six months before Chad was brought on board. He is a really nice guy. Married less than two years, has a baby girl and is just trying to make a decent living for his family. Not sure Sweeney & Todd were the wisest choice for such a decent guy. I'm not sure how long he will be able to stomach their ethics. He often worked on cases with Chad.

Cindy Curtis's little red Fiat was there. I remember pausing and marveling that it was just like her to have a completely impractical car to drive in Michigan during the winter. Wished her good luck on getting out of there that night. She was a relatively new hire, less than six months I think. She came from somewhere down South. She has an overly fake southern drawl that she tries to use to her advantage every chance she gets. I'd disliked her the moment I'd met her at the firm's Christmas party a few weeks ago. Flirting with every male there while infuriating every other female. She is a piece of work." I rolled my eyes and told Gladys I needed to take a break for a minute. I ran to the bathroom while Gladys got us some water from the kitchen.

We gathered back in the living room in front of the

large windows and just sat quietly looking out over the vast white landscape. I sighed, "Where was I? Oh in the parking garage. There were a couple other cars down there that I didn't recognize. A Subaru and a really shabby car with bond-it patches and no back bumper. I figured they must have been newer staff. I remember thinking that because they were older model cars, the one was a wreck. Usually one of the first things the attorneys at Sweeney & Todd bought when they got a few paychecks under their belt was a fancy car to impress people with. Whoever owned those cars was probably trying to make a big impression and sucking up to Chad or maybe Gary, hoping that one of them would help them climb the ladder of success to partner. The only other people the cars could have belonged to would be some of the cleaning crew. I'm not sure.

I didn't see anyone until I got up to Chad's floor. I used the employee elevator using the pass key Chad had given me so I could get off on the 7th floor that was for attorneys use only. I figured Chad would be there in his office. Sweeney & Todd also took up the entire 8th floor but that was used for partner offices and meeting rooms used to meet with clients. No one would have been up there two days before Christmas. Only the overly ambitious and suck ups would be in at all on a night snowing like it was.

The 7th floor was dim with lights only coming from five offices. The number of lit up offices matched the number of cars down below. I walked to Chad's office and nodded hello to Sara. She was startled to see me and started to say something as if to stop me but I think she could sense I was on a mission and ended up simply nodding back. I rapped on the door to Chad's office once and let myself in. I left the door open. I didn't expect it to take me too long and knew I didn't have anything to hide."

I had to pause in my retelling of that emotional night. I needed to take another breather. I went out to the kitchen to refresh our mimosas since I needed some liquid courage to get through the next recollections. Not that I dreaded rehashing the breaking up part but every time I imagined Chad sitting frozen in his chair, visions of him sitting there with an eight inch pair of scissors sticking out of his chest popped into my head. Not a pretty picture. Thanks a lot LuAnn for that indelible impression on my brain. Gladys had been taking notes and kept encouraging me to keep up the good work and to keep focusing on my instincts and impressions of those last moments I had with Chad.

"Chad had looked startled at me being there and he looked slightly disheveled. I wasn't surprised at that. He had been there over ten hours already and even though they had a gym and locker room for the attorneys to use, I was sure he hadn't taken a break. He was working on some big case for a company that was suing a major supplier out of China. It meant millions for the firm and he was hoping it would catapult him up to the 8th floor as the youngest partner in Sweeney & Todd history. It would be quite an accomplishment and a huge feather in his cap.

Chad asked me angrily what I was doing there, barging in like that. I paused, not sure exactly how to begin. I took a couple of deep breaths to compose myself and remember thinking his office really smelled funny. Like sweat mixed with a really heavy sweet perfume. I thought Sara must have just been in there and figured she wore way too much perfume. It was distracting. I pushed through my nausea, which was either from the smell or what I was about to do. I'm not exactly sure. Once I got my bearings, I simply told Chad I had decided I just couldn't take it anymore. I couldn't stand his self-centered smug attitude toward me and almost anyone he didn't consider a potential client. I told him how I felt he really had no real love for me and that I was only good as a potential trophy wife. Good enough looking and educated enough to play the part for him but obviously not good enough to commit to since we had been together over seven years and he had yet to ask me to marry him. It simply wasn't something I was willing to sacrifice myself for anymore. Frankly, I really didn't want it anymore. I told him it was over and that I had taken all my things from the house. I had loaded Hank and wouldn't be back.

Chad had just sat there. Something was off but I can't put my finger on exactly what. He seemed preoccupied and only half listened to what I was saying. He seemed to be almost holding his breath. He didn't make any move to get up at all. He did jerk once like he slipped in his chair. It made him jerk his feet under the desk. That's when I noticed the Louboutin shoes because they moved and caught my attention. I knew they were Louboutins because I could see the red soles since they were upside down."

I had to explain to Gladys that Louboutin shoes were very expensive high-end fashion shoes with signature red soles so they were easily recognizable. I admitted to regretting not snagging the shoes then since they were obviously my Christmas present. I explained to Gladys that Chad had likely picked them up on his last trip to China where they routinely sold fake products at really discounted prices. Tried to brush off knowing that because they were not in a box, too embarrassed to admit to her that I also knew Chad well enough to know he would never spend the kind of money on me that authentic Christian Louboutin's would set him back.

Gladys just kept nodding and taking notes and occasionally muttering "jerk" when I mentioned Chad's name. She encouraged me to keep recalling that night and not to leave any details out. I closed my eyes again and took myself back there.

"I had been a little distracted by the shoes and I remember staring at them. Chad had called my name to get me to look back at him. He urged me to quit being so dramatic and making rash, irrational decisions. He asked me if it was that time of the month for me (this solicited another round of 'what a jerk' and 'asshole' from Gladys). I'm sure he was just trying to figure out what was causing me to be so out of character. I had never really stood up to him before so we were having a lot of firsts. He told me to wait until he got home. Clearly he hadn't listened when I told him Hank was loaded and I wouldn't be going back there. Then he said he would finish up and be home in an hour or so. He said he loved me more than anything and then he winced, almost like he was in pain and gasped a little saying I couldn't just dump him two days before Christmas.

I cried and just hung my head saying over and over I was sorry, my mind was made up. I turned on my heel and left. I didn't even close the door. Just walked out.

Sara was at her desk and overly focused on her task of cutting out pictures for some trial storyboard she was working on. She was using a large pair of sharp scissors that ended up being the murder weapon. Sara avoided my eyes. I think she might have been embarrassed by all that she had clearly heard. I just cried as quietly as I could as I walked by and headed back to the elevator to take me to Hank and out of there."

I told Gladys how I paused before getting on the elevator and almost had a change of heart. How I turned around and walked back to Chad's office suite. "By the time I got there I was essentially sobbing and a big hot mess. Sara jumped up and stopped me from going back into Chad's office. The door was closed again and we could hear him talking to someone. He must have been on a call and had it on speaker phone because we could hear his voice and a woman's voice. If he had taken a call, he was clearly not as shook up about our breakup as I was. Made me want to slap him. I couldn't really make out what they were saying. It was too muffled so I have no idea what the conversation was. Not that I was really focusing on that anyway.

Sara had hugged me and held me for a couple minutes and told me how she had always admired me and how she thought I was so beautiful and strong. She got emotional saying Chad didn't deserve me and that I had made the best decision and did the right thing. She kissed me on the cheek and smoothed my hair turning me back towards the elevators saying I should go before he finished his conversation. She gave me a slight nudge to help me get moving. She told me she wished me all the best and that she would really love it if we could meet up sometime in the new year. I thanked her and gave her back my pass key. I wouldn't be needing it again.

That's it. I stopped in the restroom on my way to the elevator because I knew I had to look like a wreck. I took a minute to splash some cool water on my face and wipe off the smeared mascara and then I got on the elevator and left.

I really didn't have anywhere in town I could go except LuAnn's. I didn't want to rain on the kids' Christmas spirit so I decided to come up here. We had already planned to spend Christmas day up here and I figured it would do me good to have an extra day to get my happy face on. I had no idea the perfect storm, snow style, was happening. I was focused on getting my stuff cleared out of the townhouse and moving on. Hadn't really been paying attention to any weather reports. What few I did catch seemed to be the usual over sensationalizing of a few extra inches of snow. No idea they were closing the highway until I was half way up here. With nowhere to go if I turned back around, I just kept plugging away through the increasing drifts until I got here. Hank the Tank had saved me more than once. Love that vehicle.

My phone was nearly dead and I had turned it off anyway just in case Chad started calling me after he did get home. I had said all I really needed to say and didn't think it would do any good to rehash anything more with him. I didn't have any clue about his murder or Sara's attack until I got here and LuAnn filled me in."

I explained the high tech features of the house to Gladys. She was impressed with the video and audio security system and whistled saying, "I always knew they were fancy rich. They are nice down to earth folks though too. Nice combination. They aren't uppity like Chad."

We sat watching the flames in the magnificent gas fireplace contemplating my predicament when Gladys started grilling me again. "When you talked to Sara, did she smell?"

"Uhm, no actually. I don't recall smelling anything out by her office and I didn't have anything lingering on me after she hugged me."

"When you heard Chad on the phone, did you notice if her phone was all lit up? I mean those fancy secretary phones usually have more than one line and they light up when their bosses are on one. They can even have more than one line going at a time, know what I mean?"

I closed my eyes again trying to visualize being back next to Sara's desk. "She had so many papers in front of her. She had actually pushed a pile of them to the side towards the phone almost like she was trying to cover it. Sara had glanced at it and back towards Chad's door. You know, now that I think about it, I'm not sure it was lit up. But that can't be right because I definitely heard him talking to someone. I suppose he could have been listening to a video or some testimony or something but I had the distinct impression that he was conversing with someone. It had to be the phone because no one had walked past me into his office after I left. The only way in there was past the elevators and I was there the entire time."

"Did you see anyone leave his office as you were arriving?"

"No, I already told you. The only people I saw the entire time I was in the building were Chad and Sara."

Gladys looked me square in the eyes and asked bluntly, "could someone have been in there when you barged in?"

"What? No, and I didn't really barge in. I tapped on the door and opened it kinda slow, not fast like barging. Maybe I didn't allow for an appropriate amount of wait time but I wouldn't call it barging. It wasn't like I was in a rush to drop a bomb on him but I did want to get it over with. Besides, it's not like he had any closet or bathroom or anyplace for anyone to hide in there. He wouldn't get those amenities until he moved up to the 8th floor. Why would anyone hide anyway? That doesn't make any sense."

"Well missy, seems to me some odiferous woman was in there or in close proximity and if you didn't see her leaving right before you arrived, my best guess is she was still in there. She had to be hiding. I'm also guessing she might not have wanted you to see her and know what she was up to. Maybe those fancy ass red bottom shoes were hers and not so much a present for you. Think that is possible?"

I felt like Gladys had hit me between the eyes with a baseball bat. I sat there stunned, unable to form a coherent thought. It sounded ludicrous but it dawned on me that Gladys was right. The damn shoes weren't for me. The bastard. They were angled funny. And now that I think of it, they were probably three sizes too small. I wear a size 9 and those were probably a size 5 or 6 at most. Probably why they looked so dang cute. How could I have been so blind? Chad's moans and grimaces. Oh my Lord, someone was under his desk. Probably giving him a blow job while I dumped his sorry ass. Here I have been feeling so bad and sorry for ruining his day. Well, not as much as being murdered ruined it but still I have wasted time being sad someone murdered him when really I should be glad they saved me the trouble. I can't believe that asshole. The nerve. Who could have been in there? Who could have killed him?

CHAPTER 6

I NEEDED ANOTHER DRINK. I NEEDED something a little stronger than a mimosa to take the new edge off. I made us another round, moving us on to whiskey. The sobering news that some floozy had been gratifying Chad while I poured my heart and soul into breaking up with him pushed me to the limit. A little Honey Jack went down easy and helped soften the blow to my ego.

After a few of those, we were too buzzed to keep working on solving Chad's murder. It was depressing me anyway. I simply had no idea who would have killed him. I had a sneaky hunch whoever was curled up under his desk was the culprit. It had to be Cindy. The thought of that perky petite southern belle under there made my blood boil. Though, while I couldn't stand her, I couldn't actually see her killing him either. She didn't look strong enough to hurt a fly and I'm pretty sure he was more valuable to her alive than dead. If she really got lucky he might help boost her up to the 8th floor. Would she really be dumb enough to kill her best shot at getting a leg up?

We took a break to get freshened up and dressed in something more than our pajamas. We reconvened looking a bit more presentable and after we refreshed our whiskey, we moved to the dining room room table to play games and give our sleuthing a rest. Gladys was kicking my ass in Scrabble when LuAnn and the kids gave a shout out over the intercom surprising us in our alcohol-induced haze. They regaled us with a rousing rendition of "We wish you a Merry Christmas" and the kids were all excited to show us all of their presents. Lu broke the news to the kids of me being stranded up here once she had the bright idea to have me turn myself in and be under house arrest. They apparently thought that was cool. I had that fun to look forward to later, after Luke finished his holiday hoopla with his family next door. Not gonna lie, I was not looking forward to any part of the next couple days. Looking at Luke wouldn't be terrible. I just have to figure out how to look at him without him knowing I was ogling him. And I absolutely cannot not drool. That would be totally embarrassing.

Fortunately we had gotten dressed so we looked mostly presentable when everyone called. I'd tried to gussy up and put on my best happy face. My soft, forest green angora sweater accented with the pendant Gladys had given me helped, I think, but being the astute nurse that she was, LuAnn picked up on our flushed cheeks and glazed eyes. Thankfully she kept her mouth shut with the kids watching our every move. Gladys still looked almost regal with her silver hair and ivory dress. She wore the scarf I had given her and it brought out the blue in her eyes perfectly.

The kids showed us all their presents and squealed with delight when they realized they would be getting more when they were finally able to make it up north.

LuAnn shooed the kids out of the room and started grilling us about being so flushed. I almost had to get a thermometer out to prove to her we weren't coming down with something. We assured her a million times that we were fine. She gave us strict orders to eat something and drink water only for the rest of the evening. She didn't want me plastered when we had the call with Hunter later. I tried to hide rolling my eyes and was relieved when she finally said goodbye and hung up.

We turned off the intercom and decided LuAnn was probably right, more food was in order. A really nice thing about Lu, she kept a well stocked kitchen. We would not go hungry. We stuffed ourselves with ham and mashed potatoes along with cheesecake and a few petits fours. I'd have to remember to tell LuAnn we had polished off a couple bottles of champagne and a fair amount of whiskey. Bonus Christmas presents for us.

I had to walk Gladys home. We had both had a little bit too much liquid encouragement and the fresh air would do us both good. Getting through the snow drifts was a little challenging. Gladys paused as we got closer to her door, "I should warn you, my place is a bit of a shocker."

"Shocker? Why do you say that? I doubt I could be surprised by much after the week I've had."

The door stuck a little bit. I had to give it a healthy shove. I almost fell into the house and caught myself from landing in a heap. My fumbling around gave me a chance to hide my surprise. Guess Gladys was right, it was a shocker. Stuffed dead animals. Everywhere.

Very creepy how their little glass eyes seemed to be look-ing right through me, from any angle. Very unnerving. "Yikes Gladys, what in blue blazes are all these animals, birds and fish and is that a snake? You have a complete museum of natural history in here. What is going on for Pete's sake?"

"Elmer made them. I lost him and I just haven't been able to part with them. It all started when my pet rabbit Stuart died. I was so upset and despondent. Elmer just couldn't stand to see me so broken-hearted. Stuart was the first pet I ever had. We got him after we realized we could never have children. Elmer shot blanks. He always felt bad about that. He decided to take up taxidermy and preserve Stuart especially for me. That's him over there on my rocker by the window. Then Rocky, my favorite cat died, so he did him up. Well it just snowballed from there. Elmer never had the heart to actually kill anything. Well, except fish. He loved to fish. Well, up until he got the bright idea to try using dynamite in the winter. Dumbest idea ever. He threw three sticks down his fishing hole and kablooey! Lost a good shanty and all his fishing gear and had to haul himself outta there. He barely made it back to the house before the DNR and cops showed up. He stopped fishing after that. He didn't kill any of the animals he did up. He would find the poor things on his walks through the woods. He was always carting some-thing home. He had the touch and could make them look like they were back alive. Word got around about his tal-ent and people started bringing him all sorts of critters."

"Really.....well, that is certainly a unique skill that he had. Maybe since he has been gone for a while now, you could donate some of them to the museum. Let others get enjoyment out of his handiwork."

Gladys sat and looked so small and lonely. I felt instantly bad for suggesting she get rid of them. I looked around the crowded room to find anything else to talk about. I needed to change the subject before she started to cry. I spotted her large binoculars on the windowsill. "Are those night vision goggles? Do you use those?"

Gladys looked up and nodded. "Have been lately. Trying to figure out what crazy Charlie is up to over there across the lake. He has been prowling around at night an awful lot lately."

"Did you see him last night? I saw him sulking around the back of his place. I couldn't see well enough to know what he was doing. I was just using regular binoculars. I didn't think to look in Harry's hunting gear to see if he had night vision goggles in there. He probably does."

"I saw him. I am pretty sure Charlie is up to no good. I have a sense about things you know. I just hope I can figure it out before someone gets hurt."

"Hurt? Why do you say that Gladys? Has Charlie actually hurt anyone before? Isn't he just harmless?"

"Harmless? Are you nuts Lacey? He is bat-shit, uber crazy and not in a good way. He still thinks he is at war sometimes. He was in one of those overseas wars and then stationed in Korea for years before he came back here. I knew him when he was younger. He lived there when he was a kid. Was gone for years then he inherited the place when his ma died. You can see his insanity in his eyes. You can always tell true crazies by their eyes. To be honest though, I'm not sure he has ever actually hurt anyone around here before. Pretty sure he's responsible for some of the missing pets though."

"Seriously!?! That is awful. Do you think he is hurting pets now? If he is, we have to stop him! I mean, what kind of weirdo would hurt someone's pet? At Christmas even. That is just wrong."

"Years ago, I think it was Charlie that did in Doris VanWert's chihuahua. It was an annoying, yapping, ugly dog but Doris loved it. She always blamed Charlie when it came up missing. Nowadays, I believe he thinks they are a delicacy and that it is ok because he ate cats and dogs while he was in the service. He's never been quite right but after he moved back into the house, animals would just come up missing once in a while. Not enough so's anyone would really pick up on it but often enough. Then last year after his mail order bride ran away on him, he sort of snapped."

"Mail order bride? They actually do that? Did she divorce him and go back home?"

"No, she was Asian and reminded him of his glory days during the service. I think that is the only time women were ever nice to him or something. He really thought he was something when she got here. He wouldn't hardly let her out of the house. He tried to control her every move. She lasted less than six months. Rumor is that as soon as he left to get more beer one Sunday night, she snuck into one of the trunk slammers cars and is still hiding in Detroit someplace. She's never been seen again."

"Trunk slammer? Who's that?"

"Just hang around here this summer on a Sunday night. Starting around six you can hear all the trunks slamming with everyone packing up to get back to their high paying jobs in the city. Most of the folks come in from Detroit. Not many of us here year around. Anyway, Charlie went completely the rest of the way around the bend as soon as he realized she was really gone. No one blames her one bit for skedaddling out of here like she did. Of course, he blames everyone except himself. First he came around accusing all of us of helping her get away. Then he'd carry on to anyone that got within earshot how he was going to sue to get his money back. He even tried to get that shady outfit your ex-boyfriend worked for to take his case. Didn't help his disposition any when even those shysters laughed in his face. It's been over six months and he's just been festering on it ever since. It is not good to let hate and bitterness eat at you like that. Just festers and gets worse. With Charlie, no telling what worse might mean."

"Gladys, I think we need to keep a close eye on him. Maybe we should go over and look around outside his house tonight. I'll go get Harry's night vision goggles so we won't need lights. He has a bunch of hunting gear and sure that he has some. It is Christmas, Charlie will be inside and never know we were there. We might get some clues as to what he is up to. Maybe we can save someone's pet."

I ran over to see what I could find and found a couple pairs of goggles on top of his gun case. Thankfully the case with way too many firearms for my liking was locked. I'm not a fan of guns though maybe I should learn to use one if I end up needing to protect myself. I shook myself to dispel the depressing thoughts and got ready for a walk in the snow.

I'd bundled up in one of LuAnn's old puffy coats. It was short on me but I figured the navy color along with my dark green sweater and dark jeans would keep me hidden in the dark. I topped it off with a black knit cap and set off to pick up Gladys for our stroll. She came out of her house before I got there. She had dressed completely opposite of me. She had pulled a pair of white ski bib overalls over her ivory dress and had the matching white ski jacket, hat and white boots with fur trim. I guess maybe she was the smarter one. Though if she falls into a snowbank, I might not ever find her.

Dark comes early in Michigan in late December and it was pitch black when we set out. We waited until seven just to be sure everyone that was here at the lake would be in for the night. We decided to stay along the shoreline instead of cutting straight across the middle of the lake. Felt too exposed that way and the snow was too deep. At the shoreline there was a thin trail that wasn't as deep and easier to walk along. It took us a few minutes longer but felt safer going that way. Once we got to Charlie's, we saw that we had lucked out. He'd made a path through the deep snow up the hill to his house and had a rope to use as a rail up the steep slope. We could see his tracks headed out over the lake. It must be his fish shanty out about 100 yards out on the lake. Nothing else to really see even with the goggles. We crept up the path and stayed low as we made our way over to his house. He had thick coverings on all the windows like he was trying to keep the heat in. We couldn't actually see inside. We checked every window and they were all the same. We waited for a few minutes. Thinking about what to do next. We could hear him moving around inside. His cottage was so old. Sounded like the walls were paper thin.

The wind started to kick up and we were just about to leave when we heard something. Was it the wind howling? It almost sounded like someone was crying. We strained to hear but we couldn't tell. We heard a door slam and Charlie muttering about it probably turning out to be more trouble than it was worth. The television started blaring and we couldn't hear anything above the noise. We needed to get moving. Too cold to hang out here very long and we couldn't risk Charlie coming outside and discovering us crouched under his window.

CHAPTER 7

WE HAD JUST MADE IT BACK to LuAnn's and were warming by the fire when we heard a knock at the door. We must have both jumped four feet into the air. Not that we were feeling guilty or anything but what if Charlie had followed us home and was here to confront us? We both went to answer the door wondering who could be here so late on Christmas night.

I flipped on the porch light and saw Mr. Palmer and the incredible hunk Luke. Oh my gosh, I had totally forgotten about my impending house arrest. I was supposed to turn myself in. As I cracked open the door, my eyes locked with Luke's. I swear I was struck by a bolt of lightning. I could feel my face flush all the way down to my toes. My breath caught in my throat and I couldn't get a word out. I'm not sure how long I stood there frozen to the spot, staring with a dumb look on my face. Gladys came to my rescue bumping me out of the way so she could get the door open and invite them in.

She bustled them in the door while elbowing me in my side trying to break my trance. Luke was so good looking. Completely disconcerting. He was drool worthy. How in the world was I ever going to serve my time under house arrest with him here? I heard a chuckle and then LuAnn chime in over the intercom from her perch all the way back in GR. Damn technology. She probably witnessed my stupefaction and I would never hear the end of it. Great.

I quickly tried to hide my awkwardness by taking their coats and introducing LuAnn. I started to rattle on trying to explain the video setup as I shuffled everyone towards the communication room. I kept stumbling over my words. Luke had me tongue tied. Gladys glided past me and slapped me up on the back side of my head with a whispered command to snap out of it. She was right, I need to get a grip for crying out loud.

The communication room seemed a lot smaller with all of us in there. We managed to get enough chairs in there for all of us. As we got settled in, I tried to keep Gladys between Luke and me. I might melt if we actually touched each other. Even if it was just knee to knee. I couldn't risk it, especially with LuAnn as big as life on the monitor in front of us. I would really never hear the end of it if she saw me melt right in front of her. She had my new lawyer, Hunter with her. He was the first to speak up to get things started. Exchanging a few pleasantries, hoping we had all had a nice Christmas day. Gladys showed off her scarf and I was proud to show them the pendant. All in all it hadn't been that bad of a day; well, except for the realization that Chad was a cheating slimebag and I was about to be arrested, it had been ok. The alcohol had helped numb that pain though. Speaking of which, I could use a drink to help me deal with this big event of the day. Wasn't quite ready for the task of turning myself in.

Mr. Palmer had come along with Luke as a witness and made tsking noises about how sorry he was to see my life come to this. Luke tried to silence his grandfather but there was no stopping him. Murray made sure to let everyone know he had watched me grow up on this lake when my parents brought us to their small cottage. It used to be on this same lot until LuAnn and Harry were able to tear it down and build this newer, larger place. Murray wanted to make sure everyone was aware that he knew I had taken a turn down the wrong path in life when he saw my tramp stamp one day. I had been swimming in a bikini when I was thin enough to look good in one and he saw the tattoo. He had tried to warn my father to keep a tight rein on his two good looking girls but he could see then that it was too late to save me.

Luke was staring down at the floor trying to keep from busting out laughing. I could see his eyebrows raise and the definite smirk at the mention of my tramp stamp. I had to fight from blurting out that it was of a teeny tiny hummingbird. I ended up huffing a bit figuring it was none of his business. What did I care if he thought it was hilarious? He was never going to get a peek at it anyway. Luke struggled to get control and finally looked up with a blank stare. He continued with the stoic face as Murray droned on. Must be his trooper face. I'd hate to get arrested by him. Wait, I was just about to. My stomach started to churn. I might throw up. That would make a great impression I'm sure.

Thanks to the large monitor, it was easy to see LuAnn struggling not to bust a gut as well. Hunter just looked bored. He probably has had to listen to Murray plenty

over the years. Murray finally wound down and conclud-
ed with a sigh that there was no guarantee of how kids
would turn out these days. He scooted his chair closer to
Gladys and started complimenting her on her scarf and
how it matched the color of her eyes. Geesh, now I think
he was hitting on her. Shoot me now and let's get this
over with.

Hunter took charge and reminded everyone that he
was my counsel and that I would not be making any state-
ments at this time. I had agreed to be placed under volun-
tary house arrest until such time I could get to the county
court in Grand Rapids whereupon I was expected to be
bonded out of the murder charge.

I was thankful I wasn't being allowed to speak. Not
sure I could if I wanted to. My eyes welled up and I had
to gulp back tears. This was so humiliating. Luke looked
somber as he agreed to take me into his custody and that
he would assure my safe transport to Grand Rapids as
soon as the roads were passable. He said he had just re-
ceived a report from his post that it might still be another
couple days.

Hunter wrapped up the discussion advising me to stay
positive. He kept assuring me it would all work out and
that he would meet me in Grand Rapids when Luke and I
got there. He sounded confident saying he believes they
would possibly find the murderer before then. I could
only nod and wipe my tears. He said that I would be
safe with Luke. I blushed. LuAnn started smirking again.
She just had to point out that now that I was in custody, it
was safe to turn my phone back on. She said to call her to
catch up with her later. I bet she was dying to rub my face
in all of this. She was hardly able to keep from laughing
at how uncomfortable I am near Luke. I could hear the

laughter in her voice as she hung up on us saying sleep tight. I might just wait to reconnect my technology. It really hasn't been unbearable with it turned off and having to listen to her might be.

Murray agreed to walk Gladys home and it wasn't long before Luke and I were alone. I wanted to profess my innocence but remained silent while his crystal blue eyes bored through me. I finally had to hang my head to avoid his gaze. Way too distracting. Luke finally broke the silence.

"Well...." He just let the one word hang there. I truly did not know what to say. I opened and closed my mouth a few times. Pretty sure I looked like a largemouth bass out of water. Lovely. I took a deep breath and tried to start over.

"I know it looks bad and there is a lot of circumstantial evidence pointing the finger straight at me but I swear to you, I am completely innocent. Gladys and I are going to figure it out. We.." I didn't even get to finish my sentence and he cut me off.

"Wait, wait right there. You and Gladys!?! You two are going to figure it out. Are you serious? Not sure if you have noticed it or not but Gladys is a couple balls off center. Not sure she is your best Columbo to help solve your case."

"I agree she is a bit eccentric but I'm pretty sure she still has all her marbles. Or most of them anyway. Granted the stuffed menagerie is probably a little over the top but it doesn't really make her crazy. She's already helped me remember some details of my last meeting with Chad. I think we have a chance to actually solve this."

"Ok, sure, sure. Ms. Tramp Stamp Barbie and her sidekick Mrs. Looney Tunes are the cracker jack team that's gonna solve what looks to be a cut-and-dried case."

"Hold on a minute buster. Gladys isn't any Looney Tunes and my tramp stamp is none of your beeswax." Luke at least had the decency to blush and look a little contrite. Infuriatingly it added to his cuteness. He expanded his awesomeness even more by apologizing. Chad never, ever apologized even when he knew he was wrong. I wasn't used to this kind of guy.

"You are right. I am sorry. I shouldn't have said any of that. I mean, I think you are gorgeous but I shouldn't have made light of your situation, Gladys, or your inked body."

Now it was my turn to blush. Thoughts of sliding out of my jeans with Luke watching and admiring the view flashed through my mind blurring my vision. I think my toes started to curl. I had to shake my head and give myself a mental head slap. Get a grip girl. Just because Mr. Tall Dark and Handsome thinks you are gorgeous is no reason to fall apart. I mumbled a thanks for the apology and we slipped into an awkward silence.

It became decidedly more awkward when we both decided to stand up at the same time and bumped into each other. I tripped on the chair and flipped over, butt high in the air, narrowly missing bonking my head on the desk. Real smooth. Luke was quick to grab me and when he did, I am positive we both felt the shockwave when the connection went through us. We stared into each other's eyes. The air nearly crackled between us. I couldn't breathe. I started to lean in closer. He smelled so good. Warm and inviting.

The beep of the intercom broke us out of our trance. It was LuAnn wondering why she couldn't get through on my phone already. "I didn't interrupt anything did I?"

she asked innocently. I didn't tell Luke she had probably turned the security cameras back on watching our every move.

"No Lu, I haven't had a chance to plug it in and turn it on yet. Hold your horses. I'll call you back in a few minutes." I got her off the intercom and then found the switch to turn the security system completely off. That would keep her from interrupting again. With Luke here, I shouldn't be needing it anyway.

I apologized to Luke and suggested I show him around the house. We ended the tour at the spare bedroom that would be his for his stay during my confinement. "Luke, I want to thank you for going out of your way and taking your time to do this for me. And for LuAnn and Harry. She was getting pretty worried about having to go to prison for letting me hide up here. She was worried about the kids and everything. You really are going above and beyond."

Luke paused and simply said, "I don't mind. Part of the job. Besides, this might be a lot more interesting than I originally thought it was going to be."

I fumbled with words to make my getaway, "well, I guess we should get to bed." OMG, that just made it sound like I wanted to go to bed in his room with him. I could see he picked up on it by the small twitch in his lips and twinkle in his eye. "I mean we should each be going to bed in our own beds. Separate beds. Yours is in there and mine is down the hall. Way down the hall. Opposite end of the house. Way down there." I rattled on as I pointed down the hallway to my room, I gulped when I realized it wasn't really all that far. I needed to quit babbling and to shut up already. I started backing up as I was stuttering, trying to think of what to say next.

Luke lingered slightly in the doorway like he wanted to say something more. He ended up just saying good-night and softly closing his bedroom door.

CHAPTER 8

I **SLAPPED MYSELF ON THE FOREHEAD** and sighed as I shuffled down to my room. Safely inside, I didn't bother turning on the lights. I didn't really want to see my flaming cheeks in the mirror. I had been such an imbecile so many times today. Hopefully tomorrow will be a better day. I started to strip down to pull on my nightgown and had a chill run down my spine. I froze for a second. It felt like someone was looking at me. I glanced over at the camera in the corner by the ceiling. No little lights twinkling, couldn't be. I had shut the entire system down. As I nervously looked around the room, I realized the curtains were open on the window facing the lake. They really only kept the sun from shining in. With the tinting, it shouldn't matter if they were open since no one could see in. I went over to close them, peering out over the moonlit snow but I could only see shadows that looked scary in the night. I shuddered as I pulled the drapes tightly closed. I couldn't shake the feeling someone was watching me. I finished dressing in my nightgown and jumped into bed, pulling the covers up tight around me. Looks like I might be in for another long sleepless night.

If I had been thinking, I should have brought the night vision goggles up here with me so I could look across the lake and see if Charlie was out prowling around his house again tonight. If I had, and stayed at the window a little longer, I would have noticed Charlie standing out at the edge of the lake glaring back at the house.

I couldn't get to sleep. I tossed and turned for over an hour and decided to see if Gladys' trick of having some warm milk might help. Hot chocolate might help settle my mind and stomach. I wasn't used to drinking as much liquor as I had today.

I crept quietly down the stairs and into the kitchen only to find Luke already there. His head was in the fridge, leaving me a perfect view of his shirtless, very muscular back. He had on shorts that fit perfectly with what might be the finest butt I have ever seen. I just admired the view quietly as he grabbed the makings for a turkey sandwich. He didn't even blink when he turned and saw me. His abs looked like they were made of steel. Smooth as granite. My nerves were frazzled. His smile was even unnerving. I started to sweat and mumble about needing a little something to eat myself.

We made sandwiches and hot cocoa and ate at the kitchen counter with just the glow from the nightlight lighting the room. It felt warm, cozy, and comfortable. Just right. We talked easily, keeping away from tough subjects, like how a nice girl like me could end up being accused of murder. We started with the weather. Fairly benign, even though we had just survived an epic snowfall. Incredible that we were still getting snow, just not by the bucket full. Luke was amazed I'd made it up here by myself. Had to admit I couldn't have done it without Hank. Luke looked confused until I told him Hank was my 4Runner. I'd introduce him in the morning.

I loved listening to Luke tell me about how he decided to become a trooper. Said he was an eyewitness to a robbery. "I was just 16 and had just got my driver's license. Mom had given me the keys to the car so I could run to the store for her. She let me take Kenny, my best friend. We took the long way just so we could be driving around more. I remember thinking maybe we would drive by some of the girls from school that still couldn't drive and how impressed they would be. When we pulled into the grocery store parking lot, we saw two guys about our age with guns. They were climbing into a beat up Impala. Then we noticed an old woman badly beaten and struggling to get up. We stopped to help her and stayed with her until medical help arrived. Turns out she was 90 years old and had less than twenty dollars in her purse. I couldn't believe they had pummeled her so severely, all for twenty bucks.

For some reason, I had the wherewithal to remember to write down the license plate number. I was able to give a good description of the car too. They were able to pick up the assailants at a party store not too far from the grocery store. It felt good knowing I was able to help. Once I heard that the woman did not survive her injuries, I was determined to try and do more to help the innocent.

Making it through the academy was the hardest thing I have ever done. It took six months but I made it. Kenny did too. He graduated top in the class and I was second. It helped because we got to pick our posts. Kenny was my best friend since high school. We did everything together.

You would have liked him. He was better looking, stronger, faster. He always won, no matter what we did. Just like at the academy." Luke paused as if unsure how to go on.

I probed slightly. "Were you partners? Where did Kenny go? Did he go to another post?"

Luke went very still and very quiet. Staring down at the crumbs on his plate, unfocused, not really seeing what was in front of him but somewhere in his past. My heart ached watching him struggle to find the words to tell me. I stayed quiet too, giving him the time and space he needed to respond.

Luke finally took a deep breath and began. So softly, I had to lean closer in order to hear him. "We were allowed to be partners after we made it through the first couple of years. Two years ago, we were just about done with our last shift for the week. We typically work 10 hour days in a cycle of three on two off, five on four off. We were both ready for our long weekend. It had been a long run that week and we were exhausted. We had been working on an investigation that would bring down a drug cartel that had expanded into GR. We were close to being able to make arrests. Target was to take them down the following week. We were frustrated that we had to wait. We were ready but had to hold up to make sure all the legalities were in place so the arrests would stick.

"Anyway, we were cruising around burning the last hour of our shift. As we were waiting to turn out of a city parking lot, Kenny put his window down to joke with some young kids riding their bikes through the lots. He was great with kids. They loved him and they always forgot any fear they might have of law enforcement. I noticed one of them get a frightened look in his eyes and turn to speed away. That's when I saw the flash from a .38. It happened so fast. The car was surrounded. I ducked and tried to push Kenny down. I knew he was focused on the kids. They all disappeared fast and were fine."

Luke paused, grabbing a bottle of water out of the fridge and downing most of it in one gulp. He sat quietly for a couple minutes then continued, "Kenny was totally exposed. They took him out before I could blink. Only thing that saved me was another patrol that was already rolling through the area. The gang scattered when they hit their lights. We were close to the hospital so I broke all the rules and rushed Kenny to the ER. There wasn't anything they could do. He had taken a direct hit right in his brain. I was glad he never knew what hit him.

"They told me I was lucky. For whatever reason, when they shot me, they aimed low and hit me in the vest. It was supposed to be a .38 special, a cop killer that could penetrate our bullet proof vests. It did, but barely. Left me with a little scar. Right here." He pointed out the small star-shaped scar just on his chest. I wanted to reach out and touch it but I refrained myself. I didn't want to interrupt him. I waited for him to finish telling me about that agonizing day.

"The gang was part of the cartel that we were after. There was a leak and they knew we were close to shutting them down. Apprehending all the scum in that cartel was bittersweet. Losing Kenny was not worth that victory. If only they had cleared the red tape sooner, we would have had them all behind bars and it never would have happened. That was two years ago and I still don't know why I was saved, why I am the so-called lucky one. Kenny was the better trooper. It should have been me that went down that day. It haunts me every day. I know there has got to be a reason God left me here. I just haven't figured it out yet."

Luke finally looked up and said shyly, "so, now you know all my secrets." He saw my misty eyes and immediately started apologizing. "I have no idea why I just unloaded all that on you. I am so sorry."

"No please, don't apologize. I am glad you told me. I am so sorry you had to go through all that and so very sorry you lost Kenny. I wish I could have known him. He sounds like a great guy."

"He was, he really was. Miss him every day. Well, I've now kept you up nearly half the night. Perhaps we should try to get some sleep. Not that we have a big busy day tomorrow or anything. Unless you want to help me shovel snow."

I laughed. "Getting out and getting some exercise and fresh air sounds pretty good. I need it after today." We cleaned up the kitchen together and then walked upstairs and went our separate ways at the top of the staircase. At least this time I didn't make it all awkward. His warm 'Good night' helped me drift off to sleep with a smile on my face.

Linda Shoaf

CHAPTER 9

I WOKE UP FEELING MORE REFRESHED than I had in I can't remember when. I laid under the warmth of the comforter for a while savoring the feeling. When I finally hopped out of bed and pulled back the blinds, I was almost blinded by the dazzling sunshine against the clear blue sky bouncing off the abundance of crystal white snow. It was spectacular. I saw Gladys was up already and out feeding her birds. She'd told me she had a special mix for her cardinals and made sure to have plenty of peanuts for her blue jays. She must have a way with them because they didn't even seem to be afraid of her as she busily filled the feeders around her house. I had better get moving. It looked like Gladys could use a path shoveled around her house to more easily get to all of her bird feeders.

I found Luke already up and eating in the kitchen by the time I'd made myself presentable. He pointed to the pan on the stove, "there is oatmeal if you want some. I'm not much of a cook so I didn't try anything fancy."

"Perfect. Will give me energy to get through some of those drifts out there. I just saw Gladys fighting her way through the ones around her house to fill all of her bird feeders. Think I will start clearing a path there."

"Good idea. I will go clear some of the way around grandpa's place and meet you back here if that is ok. Make sure you don't try and make any sneaky getaway or anything. They will take my badge away if you do." My face must have looked stricken because he was quick to add, "just kidding, just kidding. I think I can trust you and I'm pretty sure I get to set the rules on this house arrest arrangement." Somehow, I didn't think that sounded so bad.

We both bundled up and found shovels in the garage. I introduced Luke to Hank. He was impressed with what great shape Hank was in considering he was 10 years old with over 200,000 miles under his belt. I'd inherited him from my dad who was meticulous in keeping up his cars. I'd inherited that habit from him too. It paid off because Hank was still going strong.

I made my way over to Gladys' and knocked on her door. "Shoveling service here and ready to clear the way mam."

"There you go, making me feel old again. Call me Missy or something. Mam is what they called my mother for crying out loud. Aren't you hung over or anything? I feel like I slept in a sandpit and ate a bucketful and got it in my eyes. Do you have a miracle cure or something?"

I couldn't help but chuckle. "Gladys, we stopped drinking by midafternoon yesterday, had a ton of food to absorb it and walked it off last night. Sorry, no miracle cure. Just a great night's sleep. Did me wonders."

She looked me up and down shrewdly. "Don't you be laughing at me missy. Did your arresting officer have anything to do with you getting a great night's sleep by chance? If so, you will have to give me all the details. Later though, once I am feeling more like my usual chipper self. Murray hung around after he walked me home last night and we polished off a whole bottle of my favorite moscato. Might have been two. Packed more of a wallop than I realized. And don't be raising your eyebrows at me. Murray and I haven't had a chance to talk and catch up in a long time. Nothing exciting happened. I've got to get back inside, it is freezing out here. If you want to clear a path to all my birdfeeders, that would be fantastic. Wore myself out making the rounds this morning. I'm completely tuckered out."

"You rest easy and I will take care of it. Holler if you need anything else."

It took me over an hour to get the paths to all the feeders clear. Or clear enough. I was getting too pooped for perfection. I had just stopped to take a breather when Gladys poked her head back out her door. "Lacey, come here a second. I have a favor to ask. Remember how you suggested I donate all the animals to a museum? Well I called the museum over in Mount Pleasant and they would love to have them."

"There is a museum in Mount Pleasant? And they were open the day after Christmas?"

"It is called the Museum of Cultural and Natural History at Central Michigan University. I forgot they were probably closed when I called. I lucked out that the curator was there. He only picked up the phone because he thought it was his wife. He had forgotten his cellphone at home. Said she accuses him of being the absentminded professor all the time. Anyway, he sounded like a really nice man and when I explained my collection to him, he was very interested. He said he would be happy to take it off my hands. Said he's been wanting to expand the museum and this would help him tremendously. So, I was thinking if you wanted another workout, maybe I could talk you and Luke into helping me get all of the animals out of here."

"Oh Gladys, we would be happy to! Not sure where we can put them all. Might take quite a few trips to get them all over there."

"No worries. Earl has a big trailer in his workshop out by the road. It has our Harleys in it but once we get them out, there will be plenty of room. If you can come help me tomorrow, I will make you both dinner for your trouble."

"Deal. See you tomorrow!" I ran back to LuAnn's to discover Luke had already almost finished shoveling there too. I apologized and explained what I had roped him into for tomorrow.

"Actually, I would love to help. I have always heard about Earl's taxidermy but never seen it except a glance through the windows. Should be interesting. How about we get cleaned up, get something to eat and find something to do that is a bit less exhausting."

We ended up settling on putting together a puzzle. Luke carried a table into the living room so we could sit in front of the fireplace and in front of the huge windows overlooking the lake. We admired the view in silence for a little bit, then dove into our task. As we sorted the pieces and got the puzzle to take shape, we laughed and joked. Luke was genuinely interested in FGE and what my interests were. We caught up on each other's families and discovered we had a couple shared acquaintances. One of them worked at the courthouse. I knew her from school and Luke knew her because she was a good friend of someone else. When I asked who that was, Luke paused as if he didn't want to answer.

I was kicking myself for breaking the happy mood when he spoke up, "Lynn Baxter was her name. I don't think you know her. Lynn and I were engaged. She broke it off not long after Kenny died. I don't blame her at all. Kenny was engaged to Marcy at the time. We had joked about having a double wedding to save money. Lynn and Marcy had become really good friends too. Once Kenny was gone, both Marcy and I sort of fell apart. Lynn felt like she had lost three loved ones. It was a hard time for her. So she left. She ended up marrying her law professor six months later and is now happily married with a six month old little boy."

"Oh man, I am so sorry. I didn't mean to pry. It had to have been so hard on you to lose her so soon after losing Kenny."

"It was hard. I was pretty broken up about it. Fortunately I have a job that doesn't let me be broken up and I could pour myself into it to forget. Or at least dull the pain."

We were quiet then for a while. Focused on the puzzle pieces and able to avoid looking at each other. Luke asked me about Chad. "I don't mean to pry or be insensitive but you don't seem all that broken up about your boyfriend. What is the story about you and Chad?"

Somehow it was easier to talk to Luke and open up and explain while I focused on the puzzle. "I met Chad right after he had passed the bar. He was passionate about using his law degree for helping people. He was a really great person back then. He got a job for a small firm that helped low income families with whatever legal issues they had. He loved being able to make a difference in their lives and make things better in some way. They loved him for it. The work kept coming in and word got around that Chad was one of the good guys that truly believed in helping people. He had more work than he could keep up with and never seemed to mind the hours.

I had started with FGE and it was a great job. I had to travel a lot at first. Nearly every week. It didn't seem to matter though because he was so busy too. I was almost always home for the weekend and we focused on each other then. It was a happy time.

It changed a couple years ago. I came home from a long trip and found a note on the table that said, 'down at Magoo's celebrating. Come join me when you get in'. I had no idea what we were celebrating. He hadn't said a word when we had talked on the phone. So, even though I was fighting jet lag, my curiosity got the best of me and I went to Magoo's. I found him on his fifth round of shots with a rowdy crowd of guys in suits with ties loosened or tossed aside and a few women with slightly smeared makeup and glazed eyes like they had all had a few too many drinks. He introduced me to all his new coworkers at Sweeney & Todd. Big surprise. Chad had taken a position there without even talking to me about it. I was shocked because he had always said he hated the kind of firm they were. A firm that used poor clue-less people. They pushed hyped up legal claims against anybody but especially against big corporations just to get more and more money. Money that lines the lawyers pockets before any goes to the unsuspecting clients. It's like Chad became a different person overnight. I guess I should have seen it coming but I didn't." I stood up and stretched, flexing my fingers. I went and stared out the window before setting back down at the table and continuing.

"I tried to brush it off and keep things going. I tried talking to Chad about how I felt. I tried to be happy that he was at least still passionate about his work but I had trouble being ok with the work. The money and all the things it got us was great but it was never enough for Chad. He just kept wanting more and more. Chad and I were completely disconnected. He couldn't see that he fell in love with the money more than me. He'd say he would be better and he kinda tried. It never lasted more than a day or two though. Even then he was always distracted by the next big deal. I realized it was never going to change when his last big deal came through on Thanksgiving day. It was more important than spending any time with me or our families.

So, I figured if I broke up with him now, I would be ready to start the new year with a brand new life. So much for bright ideas."

Luke put his hand over mine, making me pause and look into his eyes. All he said was, "I'm sorry you had to go through all that and that it ended up like it did." I had kept my cool up until then but I cracked. I started to sob. Luke pulled me into his arms and just let me cry it out. It was not pretty. I couldn't seem to stop. Even when I noticed I had gotten snot on his sweater, I didn't stop. I didn't realize I had so much pent up in me. The last 48 hours had been such a whirlwind and more of a pressure cooker than I had even realized. All my pent up grief and stress of breaking up with Chad, driving through the hellish storm to get here only to get slapped with murder accusations just came pouring out in tears. I cried for what seemed like forever.

Finally drained, I just kept my head on Luke's massive

chest and just sighed and hiccuped for a few minutes. As I rested, it dawned on me that this was probably the most comfortable place on the face of the earth. Warm and smelled so wonderful. No idea if it was cologne or just Luke's natural smell but whatever it was should be bottled and sold as calming essential oil. I kept my eyes closed and prayed this moment would never end.

I felt Luke looking down at me. He gently asked if I was going to be ok. I nodded my head without moving it off of his chest but I could feel him trying to look into my eyes. I finally sat up and wiped my runny nose on my sleeve and apologized for the outburst. I must have looked like a complete wreck but Luke just smiled and said I was not to worry and that he really just wanted me to be ok. I couldn't believe my ears. Not one word of criticism. No negativity at all. I could only stare at him in awe and my eyes started to well up again. Luke gently wiped the tear rolling down my cheek and lifted my chin up. His smile and eyes, they took my breath away. And then before I even knew what was happening, he pulled me into the best kiss I had ever had in my life. Toe curling good. I could have stayed that way forever. Locked into his arms and in that kiss. Soft and hard with longing at the same time. Truly magical.

Then his phone rang and startled us both. He answered it and then handed the phone to me. LuAnn had tracked me down. I had forgotten to turn on my phone. Maybe on purpose but she could never prove that. She was a bit testy. "What do you think you are doing? You can't just hide up there with your head in a snowbank forever you know. I have been waiting forever for you to call. We need to talk. Go turn on your dang phone and call me back. Now, not tomorrow, not in five hours or five minutes. Call me back right now!"

"Ok, ok. Keep your shirt on." She hung up on me. She had certainly broken the spell I was under. I looked sadly at Luke and apologized. He just smiled and gave me another kiss before saying, "you had better go and call her back or she will never leave us alone."

I couldn't help smiling. Did that mean he wanted to be alone with me? I didn't trust myself to say anything more than goodnight before fleeing upstairs to make the call back to LuAnn. I don't think it even rang before she answered.

CHAPTER 10

"WHAT HAVE YOU BEEN DO-ing? I know you didn't turn on your phone on purpose. I had to call Sheila to get Luke's number and I didn't really want to have to explain to her why I couldn't reach you on the intercom or why I so urgently needed to talk to you. Not funny that you shut the security system down. I know you are hiding from me now too. I wanted to tell you the news about Sara. Are you ok? You sound a little funny."

"Oh that is right! It has been 48 hours, has she woken up and cleared my name?!"

"Unfortunately no, not yet. Sara is still in the coma. But the nurses have filled me in on her injuries. They are really weird. She was stabbed in the neck and then her wrists were slit. The stab wound on her neck came up from under her chin so they think the attacker had to be shorter than her. I have not talked to the police yet because technically I am not supposed to know any of those details but I am sure they have got to know. Once they see you, they will know it couldn't have been you. You are way too tall. Unless you were on your knees. Which maybe if you were fighting and stabbing Chad, then her, you could have been I guess. I hadn't thought about that."

"Gee thanks sis. Ready to clear my name then throw me right back in the mud. Real nice. But it doesn't matter. Gladys and I figured out who did it. Cindy Jones. A newer attorney in the office. As Gladys made me walk her back through what happened that night, we realized there was someone there under Chad's desk the whole time I was breaking up with him. The shoes were never for me, they were on someone else. It had to be Cindy. She's definitely shorter than Sara and would easily fit under the desk. The skank. I had the impression she was too ladylike to have muscles enough to stab anyone but she must have done it. I just don't know how to prove it."

"Back up the bus. A co-worker was under his desk? Why would she be under there and why wouldn't she have poked her head out to say hello to you? That seems rude, doesn't it?"

"LuAnn, are you flippin' kidding me right now? You seriously can't imagine what she would have been doing under the desk? Haven't you ever played sexy secretary with Harry? Do I have to paint a complete picture for you?"

"Oh….I get it, I get it. What a whore. And Chad, what an asshole. Do you think she stabbed him because he said he loved you, even though he probably didn't mean it. No offense Lacey but he clearly loved himself and money more than you for a long time now. I never had the heart to tell you straight out to leave him. Personally, I'm not sorry the jerk is gone. Not that I wanted him dead but out of your life is a good thing."

"She has to have done it. We just need to get her to confess. We need to make her sweat and think the cops are on to her and she will come begging for mercy. Just like the woman that screams 'I did it, I did it' in the Perry Mason commercial."

"What is this 'we' Kemosabe? How am I supposed to make her sweat?"

"Let's think a minute. There has got to be a way."

"I know! His funeral is tomorrow. There is a viewing right before the service. I was thinking about going because you had been together so long and everything. Just wasn't sure if it would be too awkward with everyone thinking you killed him. I'm sure they don't expect you to go."

"LuAnn, I swear if I could, I would slap you right now."

"Oh, sorry. Just thinking out loud. Anyway, I will go early tomorrow and mingle. The entire office is bound to show up for the show. Most of the roads are cleared in the city so they should be able to turn out, if not for Chad, they will show up to impress the partners of their dedication. I could let it drop that Sara has come around and make them think she will be identifying the killer soon."

"Oh my gosh, that is a great idea LuAnn. If Cindy is worried that Sara will be talking to the police, she is bound to confess. I will be free and clear!"

"I'll keep you posted on what happens. How are things going up there? Getting along fabulously with your captor? Any stories to tell?"

"No Lu. No stories. Luke is genuinely a nice guy. We have talked a little bit but mostly shoveled snow. No big scoop to share with you. Be subtle tomorrow. Don't let anyone know we are on to Cindy. Call me when you get home." Fortunately I got her off the phone before she pressed me for more details on my time with Luke. I wasn't ready to share details on our kiss with anyone yet. I wanted to savor the moment by myself for a while.

I went to bed reliving my moments with Luke. He was amazing. I still felt warm and wonderful all the way down to my toes. I started thinking how great it would be that tomorrow would be my last day under house arrest. Though once I thought about it a little bit, I started to get sad. I wouldn't have any excuse to be around Luke. I liked him. Liked him a lot. Gorgeous and a great guy too. I would really like to get to know him better but once I was cleared, he would probably be glad to be rid of me.

I slept fitfully. Didn't wake up as refreshed as I did yesterday. I opened the curtains to discover It was gloomy out too. I plodded my way downstairs only to find Luke back in the kitchen. Eating pancakes while working on his computer. "Do you always get up early? Bright eyed and bushy tailed and hard at work already?"

"Most of the time. I have a case I am working on. It worked out great that grandpa wanted us all up here for the holidays. Has given me good cover while I check some things out. No one around here really knows I am a trooper. My family and I always tell people I work at Walmart. Saves getting a lot of annoying questions for gory details about accidents or who they might know that has been arrested. Guess they don't think I look like a trooper. There are more pancakes there if you want some."

I was thinking, 'no kidding, no one thinks you are a cop, you look like Adonis', fortunately I kept that thought to myself cause it would have made things awkward. I helped myself to pancakes. I couldn't stop my curiosity from asking, "a case, up here? Nothing ever happens here. Ever. This is about as backwoods quiet as it gets. What is it about?"

"Sorry. Can't really talk about it. But it isn't quite as quiet and tranquil as you might think. Unfortunately there are bad people everywhere."

"I'm sorry I shouldn't have asked. I know what you mean about bad people being everywhere. Good news for you though. LuAnn is going to put some heat on Chad's killer and we are hoping she confesses today. You should be free of your onerous duty of watching me soon."

Luke didn't look all that happy. He frowned and his brows went together as he slipped into detective mode. "What do you mean 'put some heat'? You two aren't getting in the way of the official investigation are you? LuAnn's not doing anything illegal is she?"

"No, no, nothing like that." I explained about the funeral and Cindy. Well mostly. I skipped the under the desk part and just said we knew she was in there. I figured if I mentioned the desk, unlike LuAnn he wouldn't need me to spell it out for him. No sense embarrassing myself to death this early in the morning.

He just shook his head and wished me luck. We heard a knock on the door and opened it to find Gladys ready to get busy on her house emptying task. She had a clipboard and pen in hand and let us know we would be doing all the leg work and heavy lifting while she cataloged everything for the curator. The curator had told her if she had a good list and could deliver everything before the end of the year, she could claim the donation as an itemized deduction on her taxes. She bustled us out the door reminding us to grab the shovels to clear the way to the garage first. She sounded like a mini-drill sergeant when she ordered us to 'get moving'.

Shoveling out to the large, detached garage got Luke and I all sweaty even under the gray and gloomy sky. We broke through the last snow bank just as Gladys was bringing us a bottle of water and a donut. "I thought you should take a little break and keep up your nourishment. It is going to be a long day. Might need to pace yourself. That's been one of my golden rules since I passed 75. Always remember to pace myself. Come sit down in the garage. Earl had a comfy place where he liked to come out and hide and ponder in peace and quiet." She led us into the dark garage. It was colder in here and a little musty with a smell I couldn't put my finger on. Gladys found the light switch and turned it on while going over to a thermostat and turning it up. "Might as well get it cozier in here." She spun around taking in the large space, " I'm thinking after we get the house cleared out I might tackle this mess and make me a she-shed."

The garage was bigger than her house. It had a small office type area that faced the lake and the main structure was filled to the brim with what I assumed were tanning and taxidermy supplies. Right in the middle of the garage was a big stainless steel enclosed trailer. You could see the shine under the fine layer of dust. No marks on the trailer at all except for the Harley-Davidson sticker on the back door. Gladys opened the trailer and jumped up on one of the bikes inside. "This one is mine. Earl was so proud when he bought these bikes for us. We used to go everywhere on them."

They were impressive bikes. Gladys looked like a natural up there on the bike but I still had trouble picturing her rolling down the road on it. We all looked around the garage, wondering where we were going to put the bikes so we could fill the trailer with the animals. We couldn't leave them outside. I had an idea. "I know, let's park them over in LuAnn's garage. She has a couple of open stalls. They can stay there for a while and not be in anyone's way."

"Perfect. You two get them over there. They should roll easy on the paths you have cleared. I don't think we should fire them up yet until I have a chance to check them out."

Luke looked surprised. "Gladys, you can work on the Harleys?"

"Oh sure. I used to watch Earl do it all the time. Eventually he taught me how to winterize them and get them ready to ride in the spring. He taught me lots of neat things." She pointed over at her bright blue Chevette, "how do you think blue Betsy keeps running so well? I take real good care of her. Of course she has less than 60,000 miles on her. Might still be under warranty."

I couldn't contain my surprise, "what, she has less than 60,000 miles? She has to be over 30 years old, almost 40. That is incredible."

"I don't drive much. Hardly ever in winter. I've always been lucky that nice people help out and deliver groceries when I need them. Longest trip Betsy ever made was to Grand Rapids and then only a couple times. We mostly just make runs to Remus. We maybe go to Mount Pleasant once or twice a year. Guess it takes a while for the miles to add up. Earl had a truck he used to drive but I sold that when he died. Didn't have the heart to part with his bike."

We got the bikes settled over in LuAnn's garage and went back to Gladys'. I paused at the front door before opening it to advise Luke to brace himself. He looked confused, until I opened the door. Then he looked stunned. Gobsmacked as my British friends would say. It took him a full minute to find his voice. "Wow. This is going to be quite a job."

There were dozens of different animal and bird specimens. All of them were in great shape. It was clear Earl was very talented at his hobby. We carried out a beaver, squirrels, a raccoon, a couple of skunks, a porcupine and even a family of deer (though Gladys pointed out she didn't think they were actually related, Earl had come upon the buck, doe and fawn separately in different years). We lost count of all the various types of animals tucked into her house. Earl had even preserved birds that I was tentative to touch. They all looked like they would fly away if I tried. The colors were fabulous in the oriole, blue jay, cardinal and robin. There was even a hummingbird. A stunning collection. The museum would be very pleased.

It took all day to pack them for transport and clear them all out of the house. We cleared them all except for Stuart and Rocky. Gladys couldn't bear to part with them. She did move them to a shelf in the spare room. She decided she didn't need to freak out anyone that might come to visit. Hmmm, my spidey sense kicked in. Maybe my suggestion to donate the animal collection wasn't all that spurred Gladys into action. Maybe Murray's visit the other night wouldn't be his last. Maybe he would be stopping by more often.

Gladys must have been reading my mind because she threw a dust rag at me, "here, use this and start cleaning up, clean up your mind first missy. A little early for spring cleaning but we might as well get to it". We shooed Luke out of there so he could go get cleaned up and focus on his work before dinner. Gladys and I spent another hour polishing and cleaning her house. It was small but really quaint with a great view of the lake. Funny how just one hundred feet over from LuAnn's and just a slightly different angle could make everything look so different.

We stood there admiring our work and the view. We noticed Charlie backing out of his cottage. We could see his side door from this angle. Gladys grabbed her binoculars to see what he was doing. "It looks like he is trying to keep something from slipping out the door. His lips are moving but that doesn't mean he's talking to anyone cause he talks to himself all the time. He's crazy. Like certifiable. Not mildly eccentric like me."

We watched Charlie stomp away from his house. Glancing over his shoulder like he was afraid the door wouldn't stay shut. He headed down the hill onto the lake and towards his ice shanty. He was scowling and muttering all the way. Was he up to something or just an odd duck? Hard to tell.

CHAPTER 11

GLADYS SHOOED ME OUT TO GO get cleaned up and bring Luke back for dinner. She was making us fried chicken, mashed potatoes, corn and biscuits with honey. One of her favorite comfort foods. "Figured you could use some comfort since I think they are getting the roads cleared and Luke is going to have to haul you in soon. I saw you on the news again. They were telling the public we don't have to worry about you being on the loose anymore. I can't stand those reporters. They don't know anything at all."

"Gladys, I forgot to tell you. LuAnn went to Chad's funeral today. I've got to call her and see if Cindy confessed yet."

I fished my forgotten phone out of my back pocket. Dang. Two missed calls and a text message from Lu. I called her and put her on speakerphone. "Hey Lu. Sorry for the delay. Here with Gladys tidying up her place. What did you find out at the funeral?"

"Not much there actually. I did meet Patty Mitchell. She's the receptionist on the 8th floor. She filled me in on a lot of things happening when we went back to the office."

"Back to the office? You went there? What?"

"I told her Sara had asked me to get a few things from her desk since it was going to be awhile before she would be able to come back, if she went back at all. That little white lie is all it took. She invited me to come right up. Rode with her up to the 8th floor and oohed and awed over her view there as the receptionist in the impressive lobby for their customers and she walked me down the hidden staircase to the 7th floor. Did you know that was there? Comes right out near Chad's office. Very easy to sneak down there. I pawed around Sara's desk acting like I was looking for something in particular and then declared she must have forgotten that she had taken it home already. I didn't even have to ask to see Chad's office. Patty asked if I wanted to go in. She had a key. Apparently she has a master key and can get into anyone's office. I didn't want to tell her I was looking for your shoes so I dropped my purse in front of his desk and peeked under there while I picked stuff up. They had a sheet covering the blood stains so it wasn't so bad. She said they were replacing the carpet tomorrow. I didn't see your shoes so you must be right that they really belonged to someone else."

"That doesn't sound like much to be filled in on. The stairway is interesting though."

"Give me a chance to finish. That wasn't all. Guess who is moving into Chad's office? Which is apparently the best one on the 7th floor. The one they move all the next in line for partner attorneys into. You will never guess so I'll tell you. Cindy. Other attorneys that have been there way longer are furious. Patty also knew that Cindy was having an affair of sorts with Chad too."

"Of sorts? What the heck does that mean? Wait, I don't know if I want to hear this."

"It just meant that they didn't really love each other or want to be together. It was just convenient sex. Unless she changed her mind, it doesn't add up that she would have killed him because he said he loved you. I did talk to her at the funeral. I didn't like her. She was a bitch. I fed her the line about Sara waking up and ready to talk to the police but she only raised an eyebrow. Didn't flinch more than that. She did seem to be gloating but I didn't know about the office move then. I assumed it was because she knew I was your sister and that you were going down for her crime."

"Nice Lu. I am not going down for her crime. We just need to give her a little time to think about it and get nervous. She'll crack."

Gladys piped up for the first time, "maybe you should rough her up a little bit. Really put the pressure on her."

LuAnn and I both responded with a "What?!!" at the same time. Gladys then offered us the use of her .44 magnum. Not to really hurt her of course just show her we mean business. Thank goodness Gladys couldn't get to GR in Betsy right now.

After thanking Gladys for her suggestion, we hung up and I hurried back to LuAnn's for a quick shower and to get back for dinner. My pancakes and donut chaser had worn off long ago and I was starving. Gladys' comfort food sounded really good right about now.

I didn't see Luke when I went in but did notice Charlie out on the lake as I went to grab a new outfit out of my room. I stopped to watch wishing again I had grabbed binoculars and left them up here. It looked like he was dragging a tarp behind him. It blew in the wind a little so it must not have had anything in it. Looked like it had oil or something glistening all over it. What could he have dragged down to his shanty? I was going to have to get out there and get a closer look when I had a minute. Hopefully before Luke had to take me back to GR.

We made it over to Gladys' just as she was taking the biscuits out of the oven. It smelled heavenly. Her whole house was filled with the aroma of delicious food. My stomach growled. I stopped in my tracks, embarrassed. Then, Luke's stomach growled too. We laughed and hurried to the table to dig in. I stuffed myself until I couldn't take another bite. "Gladys, that was amazing. Just what I needed. Thank you."

"No thanks necessary. I owe you two all the thanks for helping me clear everything out of here. I am so excited to have it all done. Ready to make a fresh start in the new year!" It looked like she might start to cry so Luke and I jumped up and told her to relax in her living room while we did the dishes.

It only took us a few minutes and when we got back to the living room we found Gladys sitting with lights off with her night vision goggles staring across the lake towards Charlie's. "Gladys, what on earth are you doing?" I asked her as I reached to turn on the lights. She stopped me with a loud hush and warning not to leave the lights off. If I turned them on, it would make the glasses bloom and make it impossible to see what Charlie was doing now. Apparently he was headed back out to the ice shanty. Dragging what appeared to be a loaded tarp this round. Luke asked to use her glasses for a minute and watched Charlie in silence. I noticed his jaw muscles tightening but he never said a word.

After a couple minutes Luke said, "I just remembered I have to meet someone over at the Lake Inn tonight. You ladies will have to excuse me. Lacey, could I borrow your key to the house. I will probably be late and don't want you to wait up for me. I'd feel better if you would lock up when you go to bed. If you could just tell me where the key is, I'll grab it and be on my way."

"Uhm, sure. It is in my coat pocket. Red wool coat hanging in the mud room off the garage. I'll just hang here with Gladys for a little bit and will see you in the morning."

"Great. Thanks again Gladys for the wonderful meal. Truly enjoyed it." Luke talked while backing towards the door and practically ran all the way back to LuAnn's house. He was in and out quick and we could see him headed to the Palmer's. Probably getting his truck. I should have told him he could use Hank. Would have been faster. He sure seemed in a hurry.

Gladys mused, "wonder what that boy is up to." She took up the goggles again muttering, "seems like boys are up to something all over the place."

"Gladys, let's go see if we can figure out what Charlie is doing down in his shanty so late tonight. It looks like he is dumping something in there. Let's see if we can figure out what it is. With Luke out of our way, we can sneak down there and finally catch him. If he is hurting animals, we can call the game warden in the morning."

"Good idea. Let me change into something more appropriate." She went into her room to change out of her dinner attire. A flashy floral jumpsuit circa 1960. Definitely not appropriate for sneaking up on Charlie on a frigid night with a full moon and no clouds. She came back out in a pair of black leggings, a black long sleeve

Cuddl Duds and a tight black knit cap. She looked like a mini-Ninja. She stood in front of me and asked, "do you think I should rub mascara under my eyes for camo?" and "Is that what you are wearing?"

Had to try hard not to do an eyeroll, "no Gladys. You look fine. Your outfit is perfect. My jeans and burgundy sweater aren't as perfect as your outfit but I think they will do and we don't need to waste time for me to change. I just need to go grab my night vision goggles and we are good to go."

"You are right. Let's get crackin' We might be able to nab this sucker in the act." She pulled on a black pea coat and her big black boots and was ready to go. We made a quick pit stop to grab the goggles and kept on going. I had trouble keeping up with her as we made our way down to the lake. In the moonlight, I could see remnants of our path from the other night. It seemed a little wider than the path we had made. Almost like someone else had used it recently too. I shook off the nagging feeling of foreboding and told Gladys to slow down. It's not like we were going to put out a fire.

It looked like Charlie was still busy out on the lake. We paused when we got to the edge of his property. Debating whether to climb the hill and check the house out while he was busy in the shanty or to go out there directly and see if we could catch him doing whatever he was doing, without getting caught ourselves. Climbing the hill won out. I didn't trust either Gladys or my cat-like stealth skills and was scared to death to bear the wrath of Charlie. I remembered how mad he was finding LuAnn and I on an innocent walk on the road. He would be livid if he found us out here tonight.

I should have skipped that last piece of chicken. I was

winded by the time we got to the top of the hill. I had to wait to catch my breath. It was coming out in what seemed like really loud gasps in the silence of the night. Gladys hit me and whispered, "would you be quiet! You could wake the dead with that loud breathing. Charlie can probably hear you all the way down to the lake. If he comes up here before we can clear out, there will be heck to pay for sure."

I gulped and held my breath trying to calm it and my nerves down. I listened in the sudden silence for any signs that Charlie might be on his way. Someone tapped me on my shoulder and I nearly jumped out of my skin. I was so afraid. I bumped Gladys and she whipped around with her .44 Magnum pointed at my shoulder saying, "don't move sucker, I have you covered."

We heard Luke say calmly, "Gladys put that gun down. You have it aimed at Lacey's shoulder. Not over it. Put it down and give it to me."

She looked guilty and did as she was told. Not entirely pleased but we knew we were busted. I turned around slowly. Seething just a little bit. Hard to fully express my frustration in a hushed whisper, "What in the world are you doing here? We thought you were meeting someone at the Inn, meeting over already? Don't trust your prisoner? Couldn't resist double checking up on me?"

Luke held his fingers up to his lips. Gladys and I flattened ourselves against the house. We could hear the zipper on the shanty being opened. Loud in the still moonlit night. We could see Charlie look up the hill towards the house but pretty sure he wasn't aware we were there. If he was, he would have been hollering and running up the hill. As it was, he methodically closed the shanty back up and carried his soiled tarp back with him.

Luke hustled us around the corner of the house and down the driveway. Motioning to us to stay in the tire tracks so our footprints wouldn't be so noticeable. He kept prodding us down the road. Not saying a word until we were nearly back to Murray's place. I thought Luke was gonna blow a gasket but his words came out pretty calmly. We could tell he was pretty ticked though. "First of all, I do still have a meeting to get to otherwise I would be staying and making sure you stay locked up all night. Not because I don't trust you but clearly you two need supervision. You could have been hurt or seriously hurt someone else." He pulled the .44 out of his pocket for effect and shoved it back in, "Gladys, I am keeping this for now. You should not be trying to shoot a gun like this anyway."

Gladys huffed and stood up to him (though she barely made it much past his waist), "if you had bothered to check mister, it isn't even loaded. I wasn't really going to use it on that nitwit Charlie. I was just going to scare him with it. And for your info, I know how to shoot it just fine. It does have a little bit of a kick to it but if I get braced good enough, I do just fine. I can walk home the rest of the way by myself thank you. I wore my big girl panties tonight so I will be just fine." With another huff, Gladys turned and headed back towards her place.

I couldn't help but smile. Gladys was certainly a spit-fire tonight. Luke held his hands up in surrender mode. "Ok, ok, I'm sorry for coming on so strong. You are right. I should have known you would be thinking safety first. I am just worried about you two and don't want to see either of you in any harm. I'll let both of you get yourselves home from here. Promise me you will lock up as soon as you get in. I really do have to get going for a meeting.

Take care and good night."

I hollered for Gladys to wait up for me and ran to catch up with her. I'd try to calm her down. I didn't look back or I would have seen Luke watching us walk away as he continued on to Murray's house where his Jeep was parked in the drive. He was shaking his head at us when he climbed into his Jeep. I didn't know he was trying to hurry so he could still make it to the Inn before anyone else got there or that he liked to be in position so he could hear all the conversations that he needed to. I wouldn't find all that out until later.

CHAPTER 12

GLADYS AND I STOPPED TO CHAT once we got to LuAnn's. We sat on the porch swing and watched Luke drive away. Gladys was the first to pipe up. "That sure was a close one. Not gonna lie, my heart was racing something fierce. I was afraid I was a goner. I was worried things might get mixed up and you would get blamed for killing me too. Sure, I would have known it was that rascal Luke that scared the bejesus out of me but if I was dead, I'd never be able to speak up for you. You might not have noticed but I was freaking out. I was so afraid that scoundrel Charlie was gonna come around that corner and catch us. Whew. Maybe we oughta rethink these spying missions. We don't seem to be very good at it. We got bupkis both times. I don't think my ticker can take it if we go back there."

"You're right Gladys. We can't go back there. Not to the house anyway. Although I liked Luke's tip of walking in the car tracks so no one would notice the tracks. Might be easier if we stuck to the road. There should be some nonchalant way we could meander by and get a better look in his windows. Or stroll by the ice shanty."

"Do you hear yourself Lacey? Hello, Anybody home in there?" Gladys knocked on my head to drive home the point. "I mean maybe if we had LuAnn's nerves we could do it. She crawled on her hands and knees next to Chad's spilled blood to look for a dang pair of shoes for crying out loud. That woman has balls. Let's face it Lacey, you and I are not equipped for such bravery."

"Ok, I guess we'll just have to wait to see what happens. Maybe after a good night's sleep a perfect plan B will come to us. Are you sure you can make it home ok from here?"

Gladys rolled her eyes at me, "Please, I'm not that much of a wimp." She jumped up, gave me a little wave and took off. What a lady. I hope I am a lot like her when I grow up.

I made my way upstairs slowly. Stopping to make sure the kitchen was tidied up, fluffing a couple pillows. LuAnn really had done a great job of making this a cozy cottage. All the nice high-tech amenities but it looked like an older, well loved lodge. The large leather furniture, with throws you could curl up in. A shelf of books and movie classics to keep just about anyone entertained. The Christmas tree added to the cozy feel. I would be a little sorry to have my stay come to an end. Cindy has to confess soon. I do need to get back to GR but I don't want to deal with the whole jail thing. I've got to find a place to live. I don't have to go back to work until after the first but that's not much time. I suppose I could live in the townhouse that I had shared with Chad since he won't be going back there. That would probably feel creepy though. I'd already decided to move on and I need a fresh start somewhere new.

I wound my way up to my room deep in my thoughts. I started to pull the curtains and looked over towards Gladys' house. I kept staring then it dawned on me. None of her lights were on. It didn't look like she had made it home into the house! Oh my gosh. My heart went into my throat and I turned and ran as fast as I could down the stairs. I didn't even stop to grab a coat. Just threw my feet into boots and took off running.

I got there and the front door was wide open. Pitch black inside. I called out to her, "Gladys, where are you? Are you in here? What is going on?"

That is when I heard her. Almost like a kitten mewing. "Lacey, is that you? Is he gone? Be careful."

I didn't take time to think about anything she said, I just kept in motion. Moving towards the sound of her soft voice. I found her on the floor beside her chair. The night vision goggles smashed beside her. I got her to sit up and checked her over. She had a pretty nasty gash to her head with a goose egg on the side. There was blood in a small pool on the carpet. I told her to sit still and went to grab some towels from the bathroom.

My hands were shaking as I tried to get the cut to stop bleeding. I tried to keep my voice calm, "Gladys, I don't want you to strain yourself but do you remember what happened? Who did this to you?"

Gladys looked at me with clear eyes. That was a good sign I guess. She sighed and said, "I was stupid. I thought the door looked like it had been messed with and yet I came in anyway. It was that no good Charlie. He was in a snit because he had seen the three of us on the road walking away from his place. He let me walk over here to turn on my lamp and when I did he whacked me in the head. I fell and dropped the goggles I was carrying. When he noticed them, that really set him off. He bonked me in the head with them and then smashed them on the floor a few times til they busted. He said he saw our tracks the other night, followed them back and watched us from the edge of the lake. He was so mad. He just stood there shaking for a minute. Then he turned off all the lights and started to leave. His voice was meaner than I had ever heard it before. He is a scary dude Lacey. I don't think we should mess with him. He turned around as he started out the door and glared at me. I could see his evil eyes shining in the moonlight. He said he knew we were watching him and that we had better stop or we would both seriously regret it. I suppose he is right. I sure am regretting it now." Gladys gingerly touched her head where I was trying to keep some pressure to stop the bleeding. "You don't have to worry about my head. It will be fine. Head wounds always bleed like a sieve anyway. A lot scarier looking than they really are. Just go grab me a bag of peas out of the freezer and help me into my chair, I will be fine. I just hope this doesn't mess up my hair."

I got a cloth and the peas and tried to make Gladys more comfortable. "Your hair is fine Gladys". No way I was going to tell her it looked like she had put her finger in a light socket. "We need to get to the hospital to get you checked out."

"What? Are you nuts? Do you remember where you are right now? There's no hospital right around the corner and no 24 hour med centers. It's 20 minutes to Big Rapids and 30 to Mount Pleasant and that is on a clear day. We are not going to try and haul me out on those roads to try and get me somewhere where they will tell me I am fine. With our luck we would crash and I would end up a popsicle in a snowbank and I ain't doing that."

"Ok fine, but we at least need to call LuAnn and let her check you out. And we need to call the police and have them come and have them haul in Charlie for assault. They can see the evidence here and it will be an open and shut case."

"Again, listen to yourself. I'll agree to letting LuAnn look me over. I've always wanted to see what those virtual doctor visits were like anyway. This will be cheaper. I don't have to mess with explaining it to Medicare. But there is no way we are calling the police. That would mean we wait here for deputy dimwit to show up and if we have Charlie hauled in now we will never nab him for whatever he is up to. So nip that idea in the bud right now. Help me get up. I need to go see how bad my hair is."

"Wait, wait. Ok, I will talk to Luke and let him handle this. You sit still while I see if I can lock your door." I got Gladys resettled and inspected the door. I could get it shut but could not get it to lock. No way I was letting her stay here tonight. Convincing her to come stay with me at LuAnn's wasn't as hard as I thought it was going to be. She was putting on a brave front but I could still see her shaking. I grabbed her nightgown, a few toiletries and a new outfit for the morning. "Ready to go Gladys? We should go and get you to bed. It is getting late."

She tried to smile but as she stood up, it looked more like a grimace. "Let's go, this might be fun. Kinda like a slumber party."

We carefully made our way back to LuAnn's house and I breathed a sigh of relief once we were back safe inside with the door locked. I helped Gladys into the communication room and set her up in front of the monitor before calling LuAnn. I guess I didn't think that through completely because as soon as LuAnn answered the first thing she saw Gladys' bloody head filling the screen.

LuAnn screamed the minute she saw her. "OH MY GOD!!! What the hell happened?! Lacey what the hell are you doing up there?!" So much for my badass, calm, cool and collected nurse sister.

"Whoa, hold on a sec Lu. We need your nursing expertise. Gladys was attacked by crazy Charlie and it's not like we can zip over to the hospital so we were hoping you could help. The why is a long story and I will fill you in on that later."

Fortunately my request gave her enough time to compose herself and she snapped into professional nurse mode. "Ok, Lacey, go up in my bathroom and bring down the box of sanitizing wipes, steri-strips, and a couple of wet washcloths and a towel. Gladys can fill me in on what happened while you go. Gladys, can you scoot closer to the screen and let me look into your eyes?"

I scampered off to get my supplies while Gladys obeyed and pressed her face against the monitor so LuAnn could get a better look. I could hear Gladys recounting how Charlie had been waiting for her when she walked in (thankfully omitting mentioning our attempt to spy on him and Luke taking away her gun) and how he had whacked her with the goggles. I got back as LuAnn was finishing her visual exam.

"Ok, Gladys, your eyes look clear and you seem coherent."

"Of course I am. It is gonna take a lot more than Charlie Hooper to take me down. I'm no pansy you know. Earl taught me jujitsu. Of course that was almost 60 years ago but once you have skills you never really lose them you know."

"Right, well, I'm glad to hear that. Did you lose consciousness? Feel tired, or nauseous, have a headache?"

"I don't think I blacked out. Not sure how long it took Lacey to find me though. It couldn't have been long. And of course I am tired. I'm dang near 80 and it's way past my bedtime. This whole business with Charlie makes me sick to my stomach and makes my head hurt but I'm too tired to know if it is more than that."

"Ok, I will quit pestering you. Lacey, I want you to gently wash off Gladys and then wipe the laceration on her forehead with one of the wipes." I proceeded to follow my instructions and she continued to guide me through fixing Gladys up. "Ok, good. Now open the steri-strips and try to gently hold the skin together and then apply the steri-strips to hold that together. Place one side down then pull it over to the other side to keep the wound closed. Three strips should do."

I was sweating trying to make sure I had the cut lined up right. I ended up using four strips just to be on the safe side. "There, how is that?"

Gladys leaned back towards the monitor to give LuAnn a close up view. "Are you girls just about done? I really am getting kinda tuckered out and am sure I will feel a thousand percent better if I can just get some sleep. You don't have to get the cut sealed perfectly or anything. Not like I don't have any wrinkles."

"Ok Gladys. We are done. I just want Lacey to get you settled and to put some ice on any swelling or contusions. I mean bruises. Use ice for 20 minutes then take a break from it for at least that long before applying again. Take two Tylenol now and when you get up take 2 Motrin. You can alternate between those two medications, Tylenol every two hours then Mortin every six hours as needed for pain. Lacey? Do you have that? Keep an eye on her and call me back immediately if any swelling increases or she seems worse in any way."

"Got it Lu. Thanks a million. We will talk to you tomorrow." We hung up and I helped Gladys up to the boys room. No mirrors to worry about. I helped her into her nighty and gave her the Tylenol before settling her in bed with an ice pack on her head and knees.

Gladys fidgeted and started to fuss, "Are you sure this is a good idea? I don't want this ice melting and making it seem like I wet the bed or something."

"It will be fine. I'm going to sit here for the 20 minutes we need to leave it on then I'll take it off and leave you alone. Well, I will check on you later but I promise I won't bug you with more ice tonight unless you want it." I think Gladys was out before her head hit the pillow. I sat on the small desk chair and waited for the required 20 minutes before taking off the ice packs and rearranging the blankets around Gladys. She looked so small and frail lying there. I prayed she would be ok when she woke up in the morning.

I made my way downstairs with panic setting in with every step. I couldn't remember if I had locked the door when we came in. What if Charlie had come here and was waiting to bash my head in? I ran to the kitchen and grabbed a butcher knife before checking the door. Then I went through the rest of the house pulling all the shades and making sure all the doors and windows were locked. I wish Luke hadn't taken away Gladys' gun. I hate guns but think I would feel safer with it here right now. Even without bullets. I'd feel a whole lot safer if Luke would just get back here. I know he told me not to wait up but I don't think he will blame me when I do.

CHAPTER 13

I DECIDED I COULD EITHER SLEEP ON the couch or just hop in Lu's bed since it was right next to the boy's room where I had put Gladys.. I'd wash all the bedding before I left. That was standard house rules anyway. Leave the place like you found it, clean and ready for the next house guests. I was ok with that. I tried finding something on TV and failed. Literally thousands of channels and not one that I wanted to watch or listen to. I clicked off the TV and silently waited on the couch in the near dark for Luke to come home.

I must have dozed off. I woke up with Luke sitting at my feet staring at me with a small smile on his face. When my eyes fluttered open, he gently asked me why I was on the couch and why I hadn't followed his instructions and went to bed. I wasn't supposed to wait up. I went to pull myself up and turned to glance at the clock. Almost 2:30 a.m. Luke must have stayed until closing at the Inn. The throw I had been using slipped. That was when he noticed the butcher knife that I was still clutching in my hand. "Whoa, what is up with that? Want to tell me what is going on here?"

I started to cry as soon as I started to speak. I hadn't meant to but I was so relieved he was there. The tears just started coming out. "Gladys was attacked when she went into her house earlier. I should have walked her over there but I didn't. It is all my fault. We sat on the porch swing and talked for about 10 minutes after you left and then she went towards her house and I just came in here. I fiddled around for a bit before I made it up to my room. I looked out the window and saw her lights weren't on. I knew it had been too fast for her to be in bed already. I tried running there as fast as I could. I was so scared. When I got there I found her on the floor in the dark with a big gash in her head. Charlie had been hiding in the dark waiting for her. He had seen all of us on the road after we had left his house. He was furious. He did this to her. I brought her back here. She is up in the boy's room asleep. I didn't know what else to do."

Luke had moved down so he was sitting right beside me. He took me in his arms and tried to calm me down. Assuring me he was here now and everything would be alright. My tension instantly eased but I couldn't let it go completely. I'd noticed his eyes go squinty when I mentioned Charlie. I worried he would go after him and who knew what would happen then. I pushed back and looked him in the eyes. I saw care and concern there. It touched my heart. "Luke, I hate to ask this but I saw your eyes when I mentioned Charlie. You aren't going to go out tonight and try and arrest him or anything are you? I mean, I know you could do it but that man is nuts and I just don't trust him. No telling what he would do. Promise me you won't go after him until you can get reinforcements here."

"Apologize for the lapse in my neutral face." He half smiled then his face was back to very serious again. "Charlie is the reason I went to the Inn. I shouldn't have been in such a hurry to beat him there. I should have stuck around to follow him there. It is more my fault that Gladys was left exposed than it is yours."

"Why are you following Charlie? Have you been watching his weird behavior at night too?"

"What weird behavior? Have you been watching him?"

"Well, first I noticed him going around the exterior of his house late one night. I couldn't tell what he was doing but it just felt weird. Then I discovered Gladys had been watching him too. She was sure he was up to something. She told me about rumors that he kills people's pets. We saw him dragging tarps to his fish shanty. They looked heavy on the way out and light when he came back. We just couldn't let him keep killing pets but we thought we needed some evidence to call the game warden in or something."

"Why didn't you come to me first?"

"Because, I noticed him before I had met you and then figured you wouldn't want to mess with petty game warden stuff. I sincerely had no idea he was such a nut job or that he would ever actually hurt Gladys. I am sick over it. Can you explain to me why you are interested in Charlie? Is it because of the pet killing?"

"Ok, I understand and no, it isn't because of pets. I have been trying to break another cartel. This one is really bad. They are into everything. Drugs, porn, prostitution, human trafficking, you name it. If it is bad and they can make money at it, they are heavy into it. We had a tip that Charlie was looking to get in touch with the local rep for the cartel because he had some business for them. Our informant didn't know what the deal was going to be about, just that it would go down before the end of the year. So, they sent me in because I have some connections already here and the perfect cover."

"Perfect cover as in Christmas at Murray's and your Walmart badge? If there is a local rep for the cartel, wouldn't your informant know him?"

"Our informant is closer to Charlie and knows of the dealer but doesn't really run in those circles. We aren't exactly sure who the dealer is, or where he lives. Figured he has to live in Big Rapids or Mount Pleasant. He made it here tonight so he had to drive in on M20. It is the only road around that is really driveable at the moment. A lot of the side roads only have one lane cleared so they really aren't safe to travel. Based on what I was able to overhear from his conversation with Charlie, his name is Eddie and he lives in Mount Pleasant. Eddie was bragging he'd had a chance to win big at the casino before coming over."

"How were you able to eavesdrop on Charlie without him noticing? Were you in the backroom with a tape recorder and a listening device or something?"

Luke chuckled, "no, it's not legal for me to use my James Bond equipment yet. We need more information to get a warrant. I simply sat in the booth behind them. That is why I was in such a hurry to get over to the Inn. I wanted to get there before either of them did and get myself set up."

"How did you know they would sit in the booth right by you?"

"Joey Busco owns the Inn. He is a retired trooper. He is one of the few people around here that actually knows

I am a trooper. He made sure Charlie and the dealer were seated by me. The informant talks to Joey but doesn't know he's a retired trooper and he doesn't know me. Charlie knows I am related to Murray but that is it. I noticed that Charlie came into the bar tonight acting fidgety. It was probably because of how he roughed up Gladys. Charlie gets agitated easily and was likely pretty preoccupied with thoughts of you and Gladys. He might even be worried he killed Gladys. If he thinks he did, he'll know he left prints at her house and will be caught. He is dumb enough to go back there. It was good that you had Gladys sleep here tonight."

"So was your stakeout worth it? I mean did you get what you wanted out of it or was it a waste of time?"

"I didn't get enough. Great to know his name and where he is holed up but I didn't get enough specifics on their deal. I couldn't always be watching them because that would have been too obvious. I had to try and act like I was concentrating on the football game on TV. Charlie would glance at me a few times but he was pretty preoccupied. Eddie's back was to me so I never did get to read his facial expressions much. Basically the only thing I really got from their conversation is that Eddie and his superiors are willing to take something off of Charlie's hands if a deal he has in the works doesn't pan out for him. Not much to go on. Definitely not enough to get a warrant. I hate to do it but I have to hang there every day just in case something pops up. Reality is it might be a day or two before Charlie rolls back in. We do know that Charlie likes to spend some time at the Inn a few nights a week. He likes to come in after he watches Wheel of Fortune and Jeopardy. He is addicted to watching those two shows. Thinks when he gets one answer right it proves he is a genius. He needs a lot of validation. He doesn't get it from anyone else so he tries to overcompensate. Anyway, if I can get him to drink enough, he might run on at the mouth more. He's known to talk to himself a lot too. Just need to get him loosened up and talking. It is worth a shot. Knowing what he did to Gladys, it is going to be awfully hard to resist the urge to smash him in the face."

I was flooded with relief when Luke said we would be staying around another day, maybe more. I sighed, so relieved. Feeling much better than I did when we started this conversation. I suddenly realized I was still in Luke's arms. It felt good. Safe and warm. He assumed my sigh was a signal I was dead tired. One look at Luke's face and I knew he was dead tired. I didn't bother trying to explain to him that my sigh was one of relief. I would love to stay this way the rest of the night but Luke needed to get some sleep so he could do his job. I got up and told him to hit the sack. I promised to rouse Luke if I needed his help with anything.

I reluctantly put away the butcher knife but knew we were safe with Luke in the house. I moved my sleeping spot from the couch and into Lu's bed. I was closer to Gladys upstairs so it was easier to check on her. Gladys was snoring slightly when I crept into the room. I walked slowly and softly. I didn't want to startle her. Thankfully she seemed fine. I'd get a closer look at the gash in her forehead in the morning. At least the bleeding had stopped.

I am not sure how I managed to fall asleep or how I could have slept so soundly. LuAnn's bed must be magic. I smiled to myself knowing full well it wasn't any mattress that was making me feel so comfortable. It was Luke. He was medicinal. I did not want to think about having to leave him.

CHAPTER 14

I WAS STILL ENJOYING THE COMFY bed when Gladys started to walk by and saw me. She strolled in smiling. She had two black eyes and her head was a bit Frankensteinish with the steri-strips. I was guessing she hadn't bothered to look into a mirror yet. "Good morning sunshine. I had a nightmare about Charlie last night. Don't look at me like you want to check me into the loony bin. I know it wasn't just a really bad dream because I woke up in a boys bed. My nightmare was not a nice reality. I'm not gonna lie, it scared the bejesus outta me. And I'm more than kinda bummed out that our sleuthing days are over."

"We didn't do so badly, Gladys. You were right about Cindy. She hasn't actually confessed yet but she has to. And Luke confirmed he has been after Charlie for a while so we were on the right track there."

"What did Luke say he was after him for?"

"He is arranging to sell something to a dealer. Or maybe trade. He's hoping to have the case nailed closed soon. Fingers crossed Charlie will be behind bars before the new year. Let's get downstairs and get some breakfast. Luke is probably going to want to talk to you." I gave Gladys some Motrin just in case she started to have any pain and we quickly threw on some jeans and a sweatshirt. Thankfully the sweatshirt I had grabbed for Gladys was a zip up one so we didn't have to try and get it over her head.

As usual, Luke was up working when we strolled into the kitchen. The smell of bacon and eggs was amazing. My mouth watered as I helped myself. Gladys was even starving. I took that as a good sign. Luke looked up at her and stopped. Thankfully he put on his mild mannered trooper face. She still hadn't looked into a mirror to see the full effect of Charlie's attack. I was afraid when she did see herself, she might be a bit traumatized all over again.

Gladys did pick up on his slight hesitation but attributed it to my poor taste in selecting her outfit for the day. "Don't judge me on this lackluster outfit. Miss Plain Jane here picked it out. I wasn't going to say anything 'cause I didn't want to hurt her feelings. I don't know what she was thinking. No accessories and honestly not sure there's anything I could do to jazz it up and have it match my dazzling personality." I did a mental head slap as she smoothed down her sweatshirt indignantly.

Luke smiled and asked her, "so want to tell me what happened last night? I've heard Lacey's second hand short version but if you are up to it, I'd like to hear your full version."

"I'm up to it. Honestly, I just told Lacey, if I hadn't woken up here I would have shrugged it off as a really, really bad, weird dream. There isn't too much to tell. I left Lacey and walked straight to my door. In retrospect, I realized it had been messed with but in the moment it didn't register enough to make me stop. I didn't even pause. I strolled in and went straight over to my chair by the big front window to turn on the light. I hit the switch and saw Charlie with his crazy eyes right there staring at me. I started to back up but didn't get more than a step and he came at me. He hit me right in the head really hard with something. Not sure what it was. That's what caused this." Gladys pointed at the steri-strips on her forehead that barely covered the gash. She pointed at the goose egg on the other side of her head saying, "this was from the whack with the night vision goggles. I still had them in my hand and when I fell, I dropped them. Minute Charlie saw them, he growled and picked them up. He looked through them out at the lake and then went into an even bigger rage. He bonked me in the head with them and then kept smashing them on the floor next to my head. I didn't move a muscle. I was afraid he would miss the floor and crash those things on my head again. It was throbbing like a son of a gun where he had hit me already. He was ranting that he had seen us on the road down from his place. He kept slamming those goggles on the floor over and over muttering, 'what else did she see'. He finally wore himself out breathing heavy and all. He stood up and snapped off the light and started to leave. Before he made it out the door he told me if we didn't stop that we would seriously regret it. That's it. My goggles and door lock are toast but otherwise all is fine ."

Luke raised an eyebrow at her but still didn't mention her face. Makeup might be able to hide it in a couple days. Or in a week, maybe. "Did you say anything to Charlie?"

"Nope. Figured I was safest if he thought I was dead or something so I laid perfectly still. I almost admitted to him that Lacey and I had struck out at catching him doing anything. Thought it might get me some brownie points or something but then realized they wouldn't buy me much with a crazy man that was willing to smash a $2,000 pair of night vision goggles to smithereens."

"You did good, Gladys. I am so glad you are ok." Luke avoided telling her any of his worries. Like that if Charlie thought she was dead, he might have come back to destroy the evidence. Luke had already looked and her house was still standing. "I'm going to go get you a new door knob over at Ace hardware. I think we should get your lock fixed right away. Do you want to ride along to the store with me? You don't have to get out or anything but the fresh air and ride might do you good." He also didn't tell her of his plan to take the route around the lake that would take her by Charlie's house. He was hoping with a little bit of luck, Charlie would see Gladys, realize she is alive and leave her alone.

After we ate and tidied up, we gathered up our coats and headed out to go to the store. Luke said he would drive so I thought it would be fun to tag along. Gladys called shotgun so I jumped in the back. Luke drove a vintage Jeep that had a bench seat in the front and back. Don't see those much anymore. As we were all climbing in, Gladys said to Luke, "nice ride. What's her name?"

Luke looked a little baffled then just said, "never gave it one. Jeep, I guess."

Gladys gave Luke the raspberries for not giving his vehicle any respect. "I'm surprised she is in such prime condition. I mean she's a beaut but if you don't make sure to show her the right amount of love, she might get temperamental on you. I'm just sayin'."

We climbed in and Gladys carefully buckled her seat belt. She busied herself with the radio while Luke pulled out. As she looked up, both Luke and I realized at the same time that we had totally forgotten about all of the mirrors on a vehicle. Gladys caught a glimpse of herself in the side view mirror and about lost it. "Heavens to Mergatroid! Is that me?! I look worse than the bride of Frankenstein. Good Lord. Quick! I need a bag to put over my head. Why in tarnation didn't one of you yahoos say something for crying out loud? I can't be seen in public. Lacey, swap places with me, quick. I will lay down back there until I can get out, once we are safely back in the garage."

"While the car is moving? On these terrible roads? Luke can't even pull over, the road is barely a three-track. How am I supposed to swap places with you? Can't you wait until we get there?"

Gladys looked over and realized we were driving by Charlie's house. He was out in the yard looking straight at us. Gladys flipped him the bird. Then she slipped off her seat belt and was over the seat in one smooth move. She was looking at me with glazed eyes and said, "now you do it."

I tried to reason with her. "Gladys, I am 5'10", I have a 35 inch inseam. What is yours, 26 inches? You probably did gymnastics along with your jujitsu. I don't fold like that." She picked up my foot and started pushing it over the front seat. "Gladys, slow down." For a little lady, she had quite a bit of strength when she was excited like this. She pushed my foot and I ended up kicking Luke in the head. This was totally awkward.

Thank goodness we had reached the Ace hardware store. Luke pulled to a stop in a parking space back from the building. Not like there was anyone else in the lot to worry about. Luke turned around and gave us a stern look, "you two behave and get this worked out before I get back in here." He got out of the car and walked away without looking back.

We heard the locks click. My eyes popped open bigger than saucers, "crap. I hope he did that out of habit. If we unlock the door and open it now, the car alarms will all go off. I know this from experience. Chad had locked me in once and taken the keys. I'd had no way to crack a window and the car had been sitting in the sun and I was going to bake to death. So, I'd went to crack the door to get some air and bam, weewoo, weewoo. All eyes on me, sweating and trying not to look like I was trying to steal the Beemer. Deja Vu all over again." I was starting to sweat. I didn't stop to think that this was a vintage vehicle without all the high-tech safety features. In my defense, it was hard to think clearly with a very angry near-octogenarian demanding I move, and move fast.

Again, Gladys must have read my mind. "This is a fine pickle we are in." She declared from her cozy spot on the floor. "Get moving."

"It is fine Gladys. I'll just stay here."

"You can't just sit in the backseat looking like you are back here by yourself. People are probably starting to stare at you already. Luke will look like he is driving Miss Daisy. Tongues will be wagging for sure. Now hoist your butt over the seat smooth like. Right now."

"Fine." I huffed as I tried to gracefully shimmy myself over the seat. I was anything but graceful but I made it. I had just managed to get settled in the seat when Luke returned with doorknobs in tow.

"Glad to see you ladies worked things out," he said while giving my sweaty brow a sideways glance. "I ended up buying enough knobs to change out all of your exterior doors. I had them all keyed the same so you will have one key that will open any of the doors. Is that ok, Gladys?"

We heard a muffled "sure" from the back seat. Gladys had gone into the fetal position with her face buried in the carpet. In retrospect, bringing her along was not the best idea. We needed to get her home away from prying eyes. A beat up old truck with a rag stuck in the gas tank as a cap pulled up next to Luke. I glanced over and saw Charlie climbing out. I slid down in the seat and wanted to hide on the floor like Gladys. Luke just nodded at Charlie and calmly turned on the car and drove slowly out of the parking lot.

Luke hightailed it back as much as he could considering the not-so-hot condition of the roads. He pulled into the garage space he was using at the Palmer's house. Once the Jeep was turned off, Gladys popped up and said, "is it safe to come out?"

Luke and I replied in unison, "Yes" and we could hear Gladys breathe a sigh of relief. We all started to get out and had just closed the car doors when the garage door opened up. Murray had come out to greet us. Gladys screamed so loud we all jumped. She spun and tried jumping back into the Jeep and bounced off the door. Then she spun around and buried her face against Luke's butt. She wrapped her arms around his waist in a death grip.

She had moved fast but it was too late. Murray had seen her face. "Holy Mother of God, what in heaven's name happened to you?!" Murray started approaching Luke slowly like he was afraid to take another peek. Gladys was quivering, holding on for dear life.

Luke put up the universal stop sign hand to hold Murray back. "Grandpa, no. Stay back. Give Gladys some space. She had a little accident but is fine. It really is just a little scratch and the bruises should be less noticeable around her eyes in a couple days. I'm sure she will want to see you and talk to you soon."

We could hear Gladys sob and mumble something while nodding her head. It would help if she would lift her face away from Luke's butt and loosen her grip a little bit. Luke had been trying to pry her hands open but she had them locked in place.

Murray acquiesced, saying, "ok Luke, I hear you. Can you spin Gladys around so I can talk more directly to her please?" Luke and Gladys did an awkward shuffle in baby steps so she was at least sideways to Murray. Amazingly, her grip got tighter. Murray gently put his hand on her shoulder and ignoring Luke and me said, "Gladys, I just want you to know, I think you are beautiful. Blackeyes or not and I don't give two hoots about any bump on your forehead. Other than knowing you really are ok. I'm sorry I reacted like I did. I was just surprised. You should have let me know you were hurt. I'm really sorry I wasn't there to protect you."

Gladys let go of Luke and flew into Murray's arms. "You big lug, you are the sweetest thing ever. I just didn't want to scare you away. I really haven't gotten a good look at the carnage myself. These two are on my poop list cause they never said a word. Not a word. They let me think I was just fine and dandy. I just got a quick glimpse in the side view mirror and it scared me. I was hoping to make myself less of a wreck before I saw you. It's Lacey's fault I'm in this terrible outfit. I'm just a shambles."

Murray gave her a kiss on the check. "You are perfect the way you are. Here, use my handkerchief. Do you feel well enough to let me walk you home? I'd like you to tell me what exactly happened."

Gladys blushed and hugged him again, then took his arm. She turned to Luke and I, "I'll catch up with you two later." I had the feeling we were going to be taken to the woodshed. I'd get an extra thrashing for my hasty outfit selection.

I was ignoring the tears flowing down my cheeks, not at all embarrassed because I wasn't the only one crying. I think even Luke's eyes were misty. I just nodded and glanced over at Luke. He had turned so his back was facing me. I could see a couple of wet spots on his jeans that had caught Gladys tears. Thankfully they were happy ones.

CHAPTER 15

AFTER THEY HAD GONE, LUKE and I decided we had better wait to take care of installing the doorknobs. We wanted to give Gladys some time to tell Murray about last night. Plus, Luke had some work to do and I wanted to check in with LuAnn and see if she had any good news.

I went to the communication room but decided to call her cell phone rather than use the intercom system because I didn't want to disturb Luke. Her phone just rang and rang. I was about to hang up without leaving a message when LuAnn finally answered. "Hey, sorry it took me a minute. I was wrapping up a conversation with Detective Rodriquez. He was actually nice and wanted to fill me in on the investigation. At least as much as he could. "

"Have they found anything to clear me? How is Sara? Has she woken up at all yet?"

LuAnn sighed, "No, stable, yes and no. I'll fill you in on what has been going on in a second but first, how is Gladys?"

I couldn't help but smile, "Better now that Murray is comforting her. She woke up feeling fine. Looks a little worse for wear but she is definitely nimble." I went on to fill her in on our morning escapade to get new door knobs and her budding romance with Murray. "But enough about our adventures up here, what is the latest there?"

"Rodriquez is aware of Sara's wounds and they are taking physical data from all the Sweeney & Todd employees. They believe the murderer has to be either an employee or someone like you that had easy access to the employee-only areas of the building. They are also taking everyone's fingerprints. They do have really good prints off the murder weapon and several items from Chad's office. Of course he couldn't tell me what exactly. I think I might need to pay another visit to Patty to see if I can get that info. He really couldn't tell me much except that the process is ongoing and that once you get here, they will of course need your prints and physical particulars."

I was confused. "What does that mean?"

LuAnn shrugged, "Probably just height and weight. I didn't want to grill him on everything he said. I was hoping he would spill more. One interesting thing he did let drop was that 'there are some irregularities' and that is why they have expanded the investigation and are looking for more details. He did promise to make sure to let me know if they found anything that would clear you. Technically, I don't know that he really can do that but it was nice to hear him trying to be positive and not automatically thinking you are guilty.

Sara is a mystery. She is awake but keeps her eyes shut nearly all the time whenever anyone comes in the room. They have caught her with them open. When they confront her and ask her to open them, she refuses. Well, silently she is, because she is refusing to talk to anyone. She will not speak at all. They are having a tough time figuring out why. The doctors believe she is traumatized by the attack and that she just needs more time. They are bringing in the psych team to do an evaluation tomorrow. Pray that they make some progress."

"Oh my achin' ass." I closed my eyes and put my head down on the table. "LuAnn, you are absolutely killing me. The roads will probably be clear enough for Luke to drive me to GR tomorrow afternoon. We haven't gotten anything to clear my name. What am I going to do!" My voice was getting more and more shrill. Luke poked his head into the room, "everything ok in here?" I jumped at the sound of his voice and dropped the phone.

We could hear LuAnn yelling, "Lacey, Lacey, are you there? What happened, what happened?" Luke picked up my phone and calmly told LuAnn that he had startled me and made me drop my phone. He asked her if everything was ok and if there was anything he should be made aware of. LuAnn, always smooth under pressure, told him no. All was fine. She said, "I expect I will be seeing you tomorrow, roads seem to be much better. Probably will be better and better as you get closer to town. Drive careful and I will see you when you get here. Could I speak to Lacey again please?"

Luke handed the phone back to me and mouthed 'sorry' and backed out of the room. I laid my head back down on the table and groaned into LuAnn's ear. "Shoot me now, shoot me now."

"Snap out of it Lacey. Pay attention to me. Don't despair quite yet. Let me get hold of Patty. She gave me her cell number so we could keep in touch. She might know a bit more than Detective Rodriquez cared to share.

I will call you back."

I hung up and slowly crept out of the room to find Luke. Maybe I could help him with his work and get my mind off of my sorry state. I couldn't stop thinking that I was going to be ringing in the new year from a jail cell. A pretty depressing thought.

Luke was staring at his computer but it looked like he was more lost in thought than actually working. I watched him for a moment and admired how incredibly good looking he was, even with a day's worth of whiskers. He noticed me and smiled. Made his eyes light up. Too bad I wouldn't be getting to see this inspiring vision much longer.

He looked up and caught me staring. We just looked at each other for a moment. I was struggling to keep my emotions in check. Luke finally broke the silence, "If I were to judge by the emotions rolling across your face, I would think you were on a rollercoaster Lacey. What is going on?"

I was amazed that he could read me so well. I half smiled, "well, to be honest, it looks like I am going to be headed to jail. Guess that would definitely be the low point and then I walk in here and see you and I zip right up to the highlight of the day. I am really sorry I am going to be leaving here tomorrow. I haven't minded my house arrest nearly as much as I thought I would. I was thinking I need something to help me take my mind off things so I don't keep letting gravity take me to the low points. Is there any way I can help you with your work? Even if it is to just bounce some ideas off me?"

Luke looked up at me and I was surprised when he actually said, "sure. Sit down and maybe you can help me think through how I approach my next surveillance night at the Inn. Charlie doesn't usually go every night. Joey will call me if he does show up. If Charlie stays true to form, he won't go back for a couple days so I have a little time to figure out what to do. I still don't have a warrant so I can't do any recording. I can't risk Charlie getting off on some technicality or having him accuse me of entrapment. I wish I really knew what he is up to. I need to figure out how I am going to be able to get Charlie talking and listen the entire time. Joey can help but I was thinking if I got a few drinks into Charlie and then went to the restroom or took a call, he might just sit there and talk to himself. Might just spill the beans on what he is up to. He will talk more freely if he thinks no one is close enough to hear him. I don't have the right equipment up here or the needed warrants to plant a mike so I can just listen back in the kitchen."

"I wish there was some way I could help you. I could eavesdrop on him maybe. I mean, I wouldn't want Charlie to see me but that is only because he flat out scares me to death. If there was someplace I could hide and not have him see me, maybe I could listen in."

Luke held his hands up like he wanted me to press the brakes. "Hold on a minute. I don't think I am comfortable with you being there. Charlie is unpredictable. He knows you and is probably still upset with you and Gladys. I don't know what I would do if you went and something happened to you."

"I'm not volunteering to do anything where Charlie could see me. Like I said, he scares me to death. Maybe there is someplace I could hide near wherever you are seated and I could listen in that way. What could happen to me anyway?"

"There are always a million things that can go wrong

in these kinds of operations. I wouldn't be able to live with myself if anything happened to you."

My heart skipped a beat at the husky tone of Luke's voice. Was he saying he actually cared about me? He looked up at me and I think he realized how it came out because he quickly got embarrassed and started back-tracking. "I mean, how would it look for me to include my prisoner in this operation? I might lose my badge. It, it, it...well I don't know but it would be really bad."

All I could say was 'oh'. By the way his cheeks were blazing, I'm pretty sure I had him pegged right the first time. My heart started to soar but I put on my best poker face and said, "how about we try to think of a good spot to hide. If there isn't one, I won't do it. Maybe we should call Joey and see if he has any ideas."

Luke reluctantly agreed to call him. Once he had him on the line and explained what we were trying to do, he put him on speaker phone. "Joey, I have Lacey Wheeler here with me and she would be the one that we need to hide in a secure location near enough to the bar so she can hear Charlie if both of you and I are out of earshot."

Joey's baritone voice came through loud and clear. I could hear the smile in his voice. "Hello Lacey, nice to meet you. Well, talk to you. You know what I mean. Let me think for a minute."

"Hi, Joey. Nice to meet you too. I was wondering, is there any space under the bar? I'm sure you have it full of bottles and glasses at the moment but is there any way I could lay on a shelf or something? If you do, the only potential problem might be I am 5'10" tall. It would need to be a long shelf."

Joey whistled, "you are a long drink of water. Let me measure the end of the bar, away from the kitchen and where the servers come to pick up their drinks." We could hear Joey lay down the phone and rummage through what sounded like a full junk drawer. A couple minutes later, Joey picked up the phone. "That would work great. I need to pull out the wine fridge I have stuck under there but once that is out I have at least 8' where you could lay on the bottom shelf. It is deep too, the width of the bar so there should be plenty of room for you."

Luke piped up, "there's absolutely no way Lacey can be seen by Charlie, right? I do not want to take any risks where Lacey is concerned."

Joey reassured him, "no way. There is a mirror behind all the liquor bottles behind the bar but we made sure when we put it in that customers couldn't see behind the bar, just in case we got behind and had a mess back here. To be extra safe, it would be best if Lacey could come in at 4 o'clock to get settled down there. It's not like we have a ton of customers coming in right now but it will be just Penny and I in here until 4:30. We will get it cleaned out and I will put up some towels to hide the shelf and even the staff won't know you are down there. We only have one waitress coming on for the next couple nights, one cook and one busboy. Pretty light crew. Penny and I will be the extra help and can make sure we are the only ones ever behind the bar. Should be easy. Well for us, suppose it won't be very easy laying down on that shelf til we close. Or Charlie leaves. But 9 times out of 10 we have to shoo him out of here at 2 a.m. It could be a really long night for you Lacey."

The thought of laying on a cramped shelf for up to 10 hours was not very appealing at all but if it could help Luke break the case, I was all in. "Joey, you said it was fairly wide on the shelf, so I will be able to move around some, right? Do you think I would be able to read from a Kindle under there?"

"Oh, yeah. The shelf is two feet high as well so you could probably roll over if you needed to once in a while. It really is quite roomy. Great idea thinking of hiding here. Hopefully Luke can get Charlie talking and you should be able to hear everything really good from there. I'll get the space cleared out and Luke can check it out tonight when he stops by."

"Right, see you then. Thanks Joey." Luke hung up and looked at me. I couldn't read what was going through his mind. I didn't think I should ask because he might be having second thoughts and not let me do it.

I decided diversion was probably best. "How about we grab some quick lunch since it is already one o'clock and then we can fix Gladys' door locks before you have to go."

Luke looked at me, still debating with himself. "Lacey, I love that you are willing to do this but I still have some reservations."

I took Luke's hand and held it for a minute. "It really is the best solution. I'm happy to help. Charlie will never know I am there. I will be completely safe. Honestly not thrilled with the idea of lying behind a bar, on a shelf for 10 hours but somebody needs to do it. Your only other option would be Gladys."

That made Luke laugh out loud at least, "ok, you win. Don't shoot me for caring." He leaned in so quickly and kissed me that I didn't see it coming. He was fast getting to my lips but lucky me, slow in leaving. We stayed that way until we had to come up for air. We were going to try another but we heard a knock at the door. Murray was letting himself in.

"Hey you two. I didn't interrupt anything did I? I think Gladys needs something to eat but I didn't feel right making myself at home in her kitchen and I didn't want her trying to make anything. Can you help? I left her dozing in her rocker."

"Oh sure Murray. We were just going to make some lunch. I will make something for all of us. Why don't you go back and make sure Gladys keeps resting. Luke and I will bring lunch over there in just a few minutes."

I made everyone a sandwich, grabbed some fruit, chips and bottles of water for everyone and was ready to go in less than five minutes. Luke had already gathered the tools he needed to install all of the doorknobs and was ready too. We headed over to Gladys' house agreeing not to tell her of the plan for me to hide on a bar shelf eavesdropping. No sense getting her all riled up and thinking she needed to be part of the action.

CHAPTER 16

WHILE LUKE CHANGED OUT all the door knobs, I caught Gladys up on Sara's status and LuAnn's attempt to get more info. Really hoping I would hear from her soon. Gladys said the knock on her head had set her back in thinking about solutions to my conundrum. "I feel a bit like my zip is outta my zipper if you know what I mean. Every time I get to thinking about getting you off of a murder wrap, my head starts throbbing. Usually my head hums when I am getting vibes that lead me to what is really going on but so far today, I got nothin'. I'm sorry Lacey."

"Hey, no worries Gladys. I might get lucky and hang around a couple days anyway. Luke is so busy with his case. It takes priority over babysitting me. We can tackle my case when you feel better."

"Maybe tomorrow we could run those critters over to Mount Pleasant. I've gotta get them turned in before the end of the year to get my tax credit this year. I'm sure I'll be feeling good enough for a drive. Might do us both good. Might clear our heads. I think maybe if I get some good sleep the rest of the day, we could go through the facts of your case again tomorrow too. Maybe if we walk through what we know and look at it with fresh eyes, something might pop out at us."

"I totally agree. I'm sure I will hear from LuAnn and we can add whatever she learns from Patty to the mix. Maybe it will become all clear then. We can take the trailer over and drop off your donation right after breakfast." Gladys gave me a hug and we decided to not talk about Chad's murder or me leaving anymore. I could tell she was getting tuckered out so I told her I had some things to do at the house and left her to get to her nap. Luke was finishing up the door knobs so we walked back to the house together. We were both lost in our own thoughts and didn't bother trying to make conversation. I think Luke was worried about involving me in his case and I was more worried about leaving. Leaving was going to be a lot more painful than lying on a shelf for ten hours.

It had taken longer to fix all the doors than we thought. Luke had to hurry to get to the Inn. Hanging at the bar and establishing his loner status was part of his cover. He wasn't ever sure there would be any action but needed to be there just in case. He also wanted to be able to check out the shelf situation anyway before he gave me the full green light to get involved.

I watched him pull away in his Jeep and decided I had better get hold of LuAnn to see what progress she had made today. LuAnn greeted me with excitement. Brought a smile to my face, it must mean good news. "You sound like you might have good news. Bring it on sis, I could use a burst of good news."

"I had a nice chat with Patty. Seems like there is a missing file from Chad's office. Or at least the contents of a file. Something labeled EH that was in one of Chad's high priority, eyes-only, color-coded files was found on his desk. Oddly, it was empty. A couple of the paralegals that worked exclusively with Chad admitted they had never seen the exact contents in the file but had seen it on his desk before. Apparently it was really thick when they saw it. It was something Chad wouldn't let anyone else work on. They found more than Chad's fingerprints on the file and are taking every employee's prints to identify who else handled that file. Rumor in the office is that Chad had gotten involved in a high stakes case that could have gotten him fired if the partners found out. Chad had alluded to some that he had something in the works more lucrative than being a partner."

"Why would Chad do that? Getting promoted to partner meant a lot to him. It is hard to believe he would put that at risk. It had to be really, really big if he thought it was more lucrative than being a partner. And besides, how is that good news? Having a mystery case doesn't tell us who the murderer really was."

"Chad confided in a couple people that he was about to make a killing in fees. Claimed he might go off on his own. He had been recruiting some of the staff. Quite a big deal. Partners are just now finding out about it and in a dither. Whole firm is shaken up. Worried they have rogue lawyers and a murderer amongst them. Patty was saying some are worried that if someone had their eye on Chad's prize client they might just be cold-blooded enough to murder him for it. Gotta keep our hopes up babe.

And believe it or not, that's not all. Guess what other tid-bit Patty let drop? Ok, I'll tell you and won't make you guess because I know you never will. Sara is a lesbian. She tried to hide it from most people but sounds like the entire firm knew. She had a few jealous girlfriends, in the office and out."

"Really? I had no idea. Why keep it such a secret? What was she afraid of, other than the close-minded partners?"

"Scuttlebutt is Sara didn't really care about any of the women she had flings with. They think she left Australia because of some broken relationship and had gotten into another one soon after she got here. They all say she has a mystery woman she is deeply in love with but it's someone she can't have. They don't know who it is but know she is despondent about it. Patty thinks Sara might be manic-depressive. She's sometimes giddy, happy and sometimes morose and other times very angry and resentful. She kept to herself mostly. Some like her, more hate her. The few that do like her have been trying to get her to go to counseling for months. Maybe the good that will come out of this is she'll get the help she needs."

"Oh, I hope so. Sara was always so nice to me. Has she said anything at all yet? Have the therapists helped her?"

"She's answering questions with one word responses now. Simple things like 'are you in pain? Are you hungry, thirsty, etc. When asked if she remembers the night she was attacked, she closes her eyes and simply shakes her head no. She won't give any responses when pried for any info about that night. She gets teary eyed and the doctors are sure she is remembering, just not ready to talk about it. They think she is still too traumatized. They are considering using hypnosis. They think maybe then they can get her to convey what she recalls."

"Would that really work? Could they still clear my name?"

"It could. Not clear if it would be admissible in court or not. Hunter is looking into that. It's also not going to happen fast enough to keep you from being booked in jail though. But before you get your panties in a twist, Hunter will be there and have you out on bond the minute they book you so you will not have to spend any time in the pokey."

"Thank goodness. I'm not sure what I would do if I had to go in there. Well, no definitive answers but I guess some progress. It is getting so depressing having all this hanging over my head. I'll be so glad when it is all over. I really appreciate all of your help and you letting me use the cottage. I don't know where I am going to stay once I do get back to GR. I don't think I can go back to the house. Nothing left for me there anyway."

"No worries Lacey. You can stay here while we look for a place for you. There are some cute places they just put up in Caledonia. It is a bit out of the way but not too far from FGE and it would give you a place to make a fresh start. We will figure it out. Has Luke said when he thinks he will be bringing you in?"

"We haven't really set a specific day or time. I'm guessing maybe a couple days. New Year's Eve maybe? What a great way to start the new year."

I hung up with LuAnn and decided to head to bed with my book. Needed a distraction. My head hurt from puzzling over all the latest developments. So many bits and pieces that just didn't mean anything. Sure hope everything starts making sense soon. My life depended on it.

As I got to my room I glanced out of the window with the goggles I had finally remembered to bring up. Amazing what you can see with them. It didn't look like any activity going on at Charlie's shanty tonight. Wonder what he was up to behind his closed curtains? Maybe I should take a quick walk over there by myself and see if I could find out.

I put back on my best camouflage outfit and got ready to head out into the cold night. I shivered as I snuck out of the front door. Not so much from the cold but afraid I might actually run into Charlie. I thought about what he had done to Gladys and anger blazed through me. I had to catch him in whatever he was up to. I hoped it would be enough to put him away for a long time. I made my way slowly down the road, trying to hide behind trees and blend in as much as I could. It was a cloudy night so I didn't have to worry about the moon putting a spotlight on me but I still didn't want to risk Charlie looking out and seeing me clearly. The wind howled and trees creaked making my trek seem longer and scarier than the last time Gladys and I had made our way over here. Made me wish I had thought to bring along the butcher knife. At least I would have something for protection.

I finally made it to Charlie's and put my ear up against the window of what appeared to be the living room. I could hear the TV. Sounded like Wheel of Fortune was on. Charlie was screaming at the idiot on the show for buying vowels. I heard another sound, hard to tell exactly what it was. Didn't take long for Charlie to clarify for me. He shouted to someone to "shut the hell up and stop that fucking crying! I'll give you something to cry about!" Then I heard something crash against the wall I had my ear up against. I had to cover my mouth to keep from screaming out loud. His walls must be paper thin because it felt like whatever was thrown actually hit the side of my face. I listened for a little bit more but the crying had subsided and the only sounds were the TV and Charlie trumpeting his superior intellect. I crept home wondering just who could be in there sharing Charlie's cottage and his rage.

CHAPTER 17

I WOKE TO FIND A NOTE ON THE counter from Luke. He'd be gone most of the day and was giving me a day pass on my house arrest. I guess that was fine. I needed to get Gladys over to Mount Pleasant to drop off those animals at the university anyway.

I knocked on Gladys' door and she sprung it open. "I feel so much better today!" She was bouncing on the balls of her feet. Must have been the bright red Keds she was wearing. "Come on in, I'm almost ready to go. I just gotta find some better shoes. I love these Keds. They match my outfit. But they aren't very practical in the snow. What do you think? Do you think I look like a college co-ed?" She twirled in front of me so I could get the full effect of her outfit.

I smiled, "you look perfect. I don't know if we will see many college students today. I think they are still on break." I didn't have the heart to tell her that college students didn't wear bell bottoms or vests with long fringe much these days.

Gladys stopped twirling. "Oh darn it. I was hoping we would see some of those college hunks. I texted the curator of the museum this morning and he said he'd have a couple of guys there to unload for us. I was hoping they would be like those college hunks that haul junk. Have you ever seen those signs that they stick on the poles at corners? Violet used them once. Said they were wonderful. She hired them to empty her potting shed on the hottest day of the summer. Said they got all sweaty and took off their shirts. She loved it. She said it was almost like having Chippendales right in her backyard and well worth the price she paid. I was hoping we might get some of that action for free."

I couldn't help laughing. "Too cold for them to be bare chested. Maybe we should save that excitement for this summer."

"You sure are such a wet blanket. You go hook up the trailer and I'll put on some boots so we can get going."

I was waiting in Hank when Gladys emerged ready to go. She'd managed to find a pair of red patent leather go-go boots and had added a pair of white rimmed sunglasses to hide her black eyes. I'm sure the hunks would find her irresistible.

The drive took a bit longer than usual but thankfully it was uneventful. The curator ended up having four students there to unload. Gladys was thrilled and I struggled keeping her out of their way. She'd tripped on her bell bottoms and one of the big burly guys caught her. She blushed as red as her boots and adjusted her sunglasses while she squeezed his bicep. Then she actually giggled. I needed to get her out of here.

Fortunately they were fast and Gladys didn't have any

more mishaps. The curator was ecstatic with all of the treasures Gladys had delivered. He kept exclaiming it was much more valuable of a collection than he had ever imagined. He gave Gladys her receipt and assured her he would be in touch to let her know when the grand opening of the new wing was scheduled. He even wanted her to come as the guest of honor. Gladys was thrilled.

And apparently starving because she told the curator we had to get moving and practically ran and jumped into Hank asking, "Can we go to that old fashioned drive-in place just up on the corner near here? We can eat in the truck and watch traffic on Mission street. See what is happening in the big city. They have really good gyros and onion rings and they make an ice cream float with ginger ale. That's what I want."

It was only 11 but Jon's Country Burgers was open so I pulled in. It was a little awkward to park with the trailer but I was able to pull through and take up two slots. I had to hop out and place the order in the intercom box and the waitress was confused when she brought out the order but it worked just fine.

Gladys got comfy and pulled off her sunglasses as we settled in with our food, munching and watching cars go by. Gladys sighed, "that was fun wasn't it? I think one of those boys liked me. Maybe. He was definitely cute and not sore on the eyes. Would like to see him with his shirt off. Maybe I could get his name and number and see if he would do some yard work this summer."

I rolled my eyes and almost choked on my gyro. I was glad to have the distraction of eating to save me from responding. Gladys was focused on her onion rings and didn't notice. We ate in silence for a little bit, not much going on today on the main drag of Mount P.

"Look at that fancy car." Gladys pointed towards the gas station across the street where a shiny black Escalade with spinning hubcaps was pulling up to a pump. We watched as the driver got out to fill his tank. He walked around the vehicle while his tank filled, kicking off the buildup of snow from his chrome mud flaps. He glanced over his shoulder and paused when he noticed Gladys and I staring at him. He stood there defiantly, his eyes going into angry slits. "Oops, busted staring." Gladys says while slipping back on her sunglasses. As if that would make us less noticeable. All it did was make the scary man burst out laughing. He tapped his passenger window and was pointing towards us, still laughing.

Gladys stuck her tongue out at him. He stopped laughing and glared at us. He looked pissed. He probably wasn't used to anyone sticking their tongue out at him. At least to his face. I tried to keep the calm in my voice, "Oh, oh. Gladys, just sit still and look away. Please."

She turned her head towards me slightly, "I can still watch him and he won't be able to tell. You just act like you are talking to me and you can keep an eye out too."

While we were nervously trying not to be too obvious about still looking, a beat-up old car without a back bumper pulled up alongside the Escalade. The driver rolled down his window and was talking to Mr. Scary. Probably some poor student admiring the fancy Escalade. He glanced back at us for a moment then focused on the car beside him. I was a little amazed Mr. Scary was giving him any attention at all. He managed to look even angrier by the time the small beater car pulled away. It swung onto Bellows and made a quick right so we could clearly see the driver as he headed north. It was almost like he slowed down a touch to look over at us. I knew that face from somewhere. Why did he look so familiar? I could see a spark of recognition in his eyes too. He was gone before I could put my finger on it and Mr. Scary was back staring at us. He put his arm up and had his hand with his finger pointing at us like a gun. He never blinked when he pulled down his thumb as if he was shooting us. We were staring but couldn't stop in our fear. He turned and got back in the Escalade and pulled out, making a left right in front of a couple cars. He headed south and we watched until he was out of sight.

Guess that means we would go north. I didn't want to run into him again.

Gladys finished up and asked if we could go hit the casino before we went home. "I love going there but don't get there very often. Violet thinks it makes her feel like we're floozies. She can be a little uptight sometimes. I hate to waste this great outfit. I might get lucky and catch the eye of some big players."

The casino was north and east so fine by me if we went that way. I headed down Bellows and figured we could go in the back way. I was still shaking a little from the weird encounter with Mr. Scary and didn't feel like running into him or the kid with the beat-up car. Easier to stick to less traveled streets while hauling the trailer anyway. It wasn't quite as clear as Mission but passable.

I had to wait for a couple cars to turn left at Isabella road. This trailer was a nuisance. I wouldn't be able to park in the parking garage at the Casino. I'd have to drop Gladys off at the main door and then find a space. As I turned right onto East Broadway, I could see a big black vehicle up ahead turning into the casino. I said a small prayer that it wasn't the same big black Escalade driven by Mr. Scary and prayed that Gladys wouldn't spot it as well. She didn't seem to. She just kept prattling on about finding a lucky slot machine. She had forty dollars and wanted to make her fortune before we had to head home.

As I dropped Gladys off at the door, I admonished her to wait right there for me while I parked Hank and the trailer. I also reminded her we had to leave by two o'clock since I didn't want to haul this rig in the dark. As the door closed, I could see Gladys running to the door and taking off at a near run down the hallway to the casino floor to make her fortune. I knew there was no way she was listening to me.

I found a parking spot at the farthest end of the lot, right next to the Mt. Everest of snow they had built with all of the snow cleared from the lots. It would be June before it melted down. I trudged to the casino hoping I would get lucky. Lucky enough to find Gladys and doubly lucky if she had already blown through her forty bucks and was ready to head home. I didn't really have a huge desire to go into a smoky casino and have to get my coat dry cleaned. My mood was darkening the closer I got to the door.

Linda Shoaf

CHAPTER 18

I STOMPED THE SNOW OFF MY BOOTS on the rug by the door and headed down the hall. Eyes scanning the concert posters. Some pretty big name talent shows up here. Might have to come over in the summer sometime and check it out. I asked the guy standing at the entrance if he had seen a little old woman looking for the penny slots. I should have known I was in for trouble when he laughed and said, "In white sunglasses?" Then he pointed me in the right direction and wished me luck. Somehow I didn't think I was gonna be so lucky.

I walked into the darkened casino and let my eyes adjust in the hazy smoke-filled room to the glow of the neon lights from the slot machines. I looked down every row, amazed to see most of the seats were occupied. By the looks of some of the players, they could have been snowed in here since the storm first hit. I wondered if they knew or cared what day it was or even if the roads had been cleared. I made my way through row upon row of slot machines and could not find Gladys. Amazed because how hard could it be to spot a little old lady wearing white sunglasses inside a casino? I was about to give up on ever finding her when I heard her. Oh no, what now?

I hurried towards the growing commotion that seemed to be coming from the VIP players section. Gladys was giving the bouncer the raspberries that she had every right to be in there. He was very stoic and just stood with his arms across his massive chest baring her entry into the room. I stepped up and put my hand on Gladys' shoulder, "hey there you are. Come with me, I've got something to show you." I was lying through my teeth but had my fingers crossed so pretty sure it didn't count. I had to practically drag her through the growing crowd. I whispered through clenched teeth, "Gladys, what in God's name were you doing? Forty bucks doesn't qualify you for a seat in the VIP game room. Those guys play with real money. Big bucks."

"I know that. I was trying to keep my eye on that Mr. Scary guy we saw earlier with the fancy car at that gas station. He's in there. I saw him walk right in, they didn't stop him. I think they are profiling. How do they know I only have forty dollars? I could be loaded. I think that big oaf at the door has a thing against the older wiser generation. He didn't look too bright. Maybe we could go back there and you could distract him while I sneak inside."

"No, you are not sneaking inside. Mr. Scary probably already saw you. We do not need any more trouble. Let's go, we need to get out of here." I turned to look back at Gladys and wasn't watching where I was going. I slammed right into someone. I started to blubber out an apology and looked into the face of the victim of my carelessness. I sucked in my breath and was startled into silence. It was Dexter Baker. The intern that was working at Sweeney & Todd. Suddenly it dawned on me that he was the one in the beat up car at the gas station earlier. He smirked as he saw the lights click on fully for me. It was Dexter's car in the parking garage the night Chad was killed. He was there. What was he doing here? What was he talking to the man in the Escalade about earlier? I tried to hide my unease and started talking too fast with exaggerated niceness, "why Dexter, fancy meeting you here. You remember me don't you? Lacey Wheeler. Let me introduce you to my friend Gladys Peabody. Gladys, this is Dexter Baker. He worked with Chad at Sweeney & Todd."

"Dexter, pleased to meet you. What brings you all the way up here to Mount Pleasant?" Gladys sounded like a nice old lady but she could bore a hole through him with the evil eye she was giving him. I tried to give her a nudge.

Dexter still had a bit of a smirk when he replied, "nice to meet you Mrs. Peabody. I actually went to pre-law here at Central and have a few acquaintances still in the area. It is always good to maintain your contacts. Never know who might be a potential client. Something Chad taught me." He turned and looked me straight in the eyes, "I hear you might be needing a good lawyer Lacey. It's too bad about Chad. Maybe you are in the market for a new steady man squeeze. Hmm, We just might be a more perfect match babe."

I was a little stunned and at a loss for words. I opened my mouth trying to think of something appropriate to say. Nothing came out. Gladys came to my rescue and spoke up, "It is too bad about Chad. That's what happens though. Karma will get you every time. Chad was a jerk. Jerks always get what they have coming to them. Always. As you shall sow, so shall you reap. Isn't that what the good book says?" She leveled her steely eyes on him. "And Lacey already has Hunter Jackson representing her and a way way better squeeze than you, so you can quit licking your chops. She doesn't really even need Hunter though. They have a bead on the real killer and expect to make an arrest very soon."

Dexter's eyes widened, "oh really. I hadn't heard that. Who do they think did it if it wasn't Lacey?"

Gladys looked shrewdly at Dexter, "wouldn't you like to know? Well, wait, I guess maybe you already do." She just smirked at him as she watched his jaw drop.

I stepped between them trying to diffuse the growing tension. "We have to get going Dexter. It was good seeing you. Have a Happy New Year. Bye." I pulled Gladys towards the ladies room so we could escape any more of his scrutiny. "What were you doing? They aren't arresting anyone besides me any time soon. I'm surprised your nose didn't grow while you were spinning that lie."

"Oh look who's talking, little Miss Liar Liar Pants are on Fire. You pulled me away telling me you had something to show me. Pretty sure that was a big fat lie. We need to go back there and see if that slime Dexter is going to meet up with Mr. Scary again. Maybe they are up to something."

"So what if they are? It isn't any of our beeswax. We are going to pee and then hit the road. That's it. Go fast so we can get going." I went into a stall and Gladys mumbled something and went in one several down the row from me. Just as well, I didn't need to hear her doing her business. I did mine and slowly washed my hands waiting for her to come out. I'd washed and dried and still no Gladys. I tried discreetly checking under stalls to see if I could see her go-go boots while I called out to her. Are you kidding me? Was she holding her feet up so I couldn't find her? Unbelievable. I huffed and went to the door to wait.

A middle aged woman had been watching me. She asked if I was looking for the little old lady in the fringe dress. I explained I was looking for the little old lady in bell bottoms, a fringe vest and red go-go-boots and white sunglasses. She said, "yeah, same one. She took off the bell bottoms and threw them in the trash can over there. She just wore the vest as a dress. She went back out into the casino and asked me to wish her luck."

I was running back towards the VIP area before she finished the sentence. When I found Gladys, I was going to strangle her. I slid to a stop in front of the sumo wrestler sized doorman. I didn't see Gladys being held at bay. I tried not to look too awkward or obvious as I tried to peek into the room. He glanced at me and shook his head no. Wonder if he meant, no Gladys, no looking, no talking. Hard to tell. His face was carved out of stone. I heard a woman laugh a little hysterically in the VIP room. Gladys. I put my head in my hands and walked back to the closest row of slots to hide and wait until she bounced out of there, either on her own or thrown out.

I didn't have to wait long. She came out on the arms of two good looking men gazing up into their eyes and smiling all coquettishly. Good grief. They each kissed her on the cheek and gave her a poker chip wishing her good luck. She gave a dainty wave and then scooted over to where she saw me peeking out from behind a slot machine.

"I wasn't able to observe much. Dexter and Mr. Scary were leaving when I got in there. I don't think they saw me. At least I am pretty sure they didn't notice me."

"Gladys, I find that very hard to believe. Look at you. You are dressed in red patent leather go-go boots and a fringe vest for a dress. You can see your white undies. Pretty sure everyone here has noticed you. Let's see if we can retrieve your bell bottoms from the trash can and get you home. You can fill me in on what you gleaned from your mission back there on the way home."

"Hey, hey, do not mock my undies. These are one of my fancy pairs. Did you notice the lace? They do not make undies like these anymore. Besides, they are my lucky undies. I've had them since 1959, I only wear them when I wanna get lucky. I guess maybe I should have worn them more often now that I think about it. Hate to wear them out though. Let me cash in these chips before we go. 500 bucks. Sweet guys. They were very helpful."

"Why in the world did they give you 500 dollars?!"

"They said I brought them luck. I guess the gentlemen they were playing cards with were distracted when I walked in and messed up their hands. They both won pretty big I guess and wanted to thank me. The guys that lost seemed like sore losers and not too happy."

Why was I not surprised? I found Gladys's bell bottoms on top of the trash can. Luckily no one had taken them or dumped anything else in the trash since she put them there. I shook them out and held them under the hand dryer to kill any lingering cooties. She pulled them on and scurried out with her chips to go cash them in. I hurried after her, determined not to let her out of my sight again. She was going to have to walk out to Hank or I would have to carry her. I was not leaving her to wait for me. That would never work.

Gladys was so giddy with her "winnings" she practically skipped out to Hank. I got her buckled in and thankfully headed for home. She filled me in on her VIP excursion while we drove. "I know you are probably mad at me Lacey but I had to try to go in there. I did learn Mr. Scary's name, Eddie Hawkins. Larry and Pete, my friends, told me I should steer clear of him. Guess he is a really bad guy and everyone keeps their distance as much as they can. Apparently he has quite a temper and gets mad easily. I almost told them I know but I didn't want to tarnish my classy image with them by telling them it was because he got mad and pretended to shoot us just because I stuck my tongue out at him."

I gripped the wheel tighter and kept quiet. Luke would be furious if he knew we had a run in with Eddie Hawkins. The cartel kingpin that he was trying to take down. How in the world did we get messed up so much today? I stewed the entire way home on what I would tell Luke. There was no way he was going to believe that Eddie never noticed Gladys in her white granny undies and a long fringe vest strolling into the VIP players room in her red go-go boots. I decided I couldn't tell him anything. I'm sure there was no real harm done. Couldn't be, could there? It was definitely odd that Dexter was connected to him in some way. Too much to think about. I was glad that Gladys got bored of the snowy scenery and fell asleep. Saved me from having to hash through all my jumble of thoughts with her. We could save that for tomorrow.

I got Gladys safely tucked back in at her place. She was pretty tuckered out; almost back asleep in her chair by the time I made it to the door. I locked her in and put the spare key Luke had made in my pocket. He was thoughtful and made a couple so we could both have one and check on her if we needed to.

My luck was improving. I didn't have to face Luke when I got back. He'd left a note saying not to wait up since he would be working late again. Perfect. I had sort of hoped we might have a quiet evening alone and I could pretend all my problems were just my overactive imagination. Guess that wasn't going to happen. Depressingly, a quiet night alone with Luke wasn't likely to happen ever. I didn't want to think about that now either. I went upstairs to draw a bath and make sure the Kindle was charged for a quiet night reading. Anything to take my mind away from the craziness that kept popping up around me.

Linda Shoaf

CHAPTER 19

I WOKE UP WITH A JOLT. HEART RAC-ing, disoriented and not sure where I even was. I took stock. The Kindle laid on across my chest. Oh right, I'd soaked in the tub until I was pruny then was going to read. Had I even read anything at all? I was so tired after my bath I think I was half asleep before I even hit the bed. I shook my head to clear some of the cobwebs away. I was jolted out of my daze by the incessant ringing of the doorbell. I jumped up and tripped while trying to pull on some jeans. The bell kept ringing on and on all through the house. Who in the world could be out there at this time of the morning? Why wasn't Luke answering it?

I made it to the door and yanked it open with a huff. "Gladys! What in the world are you doing?"

She stood there resplendent in a hot pink velor track-suit, rhinestone studded sunglasses and fuschia bright lips. "What took you so dang long? I've been standing here forever. It's freezing out here." She pushed past me into the foyer and started jumping out of her boots.

"Where is your coat?"

"I didn't think I needed it. Thought I'd be dashing over here and in the door before the cold had a chance to hit me. Never expected you to be wasting the day away lollygagging in bed. It is almost 9 o'clock for heaven's sake. We've got a big day ahead of us. We gotta get crackin'. Look what I found in Earl's office." She pointed to a good sized white board still propped up on the porch.

I was surprised she managed to lug it over here by herself. Again, she read my mind. "Luke carried it over for me. He stopped by with Murray for breakfast this morning. Best eye candy breakfast ever. They sure are good looking."

I smiled thinking of Luke and his drop dead gorgeous looks. "You got that right. I am so sorry I missed it. So what are we doing with the white board?"

Gladys dropped the huge grocery bag she had over her shoulder and started rummaging through it. She held up board markers and several packs of Post-it-Notes. "You gotta love that Family Dollar they put in. They have a little bit of everything you need in there. Murray ran me up there when they opened at 8. I got us some supplies so we can work on your murder mystery. I even picked up these sunglasses and lipstick in the clearance aisle. Aren't they great?"

They were certainly something alright. Lips so bright they were a bit distracting. They did match the track suit though.

"And you will never guess what Violet told me this morning. Not in a million years. I'm trending on YouTube! Whatever that is. Apparently someone got some great pictures of me at the casino yesterday and I am all the rage. How cool is that? Can we go again? Maybe you could film me with Larry and Pete in the VIP area. I might get quite a following. What do you think?"

I just stared at her stunned. Though seriously, I should not be surprised. A little old lady scrambling around the casino in red go-go boots, white undies under a red fringe vest with the ensemble complimented with a flashy pair of white sunglasses was quite a sight. Unbelievable. She didn't seem to mind. She was ready to bark out some orders.

"Grab that board and let's get it set up in the living room. We need to lay out all the clues we have and connect the dots. I'm sure the answer is staring us right in the face. We just haven't focused in on it properly yet. It is sort of like those Where's Waldo kids books. You can stare at it for hours and never see him then once you do it is plain as day and you can't believe you ever missed seeing him all over the page."

I grabbed the white board and hauled it into the living room. Might as well make this our office for the day. Gladys dragged her bag into the room and started setting up her supplies on the coffee table. I went to the kitchen to fix a quick breakfast. Too bad Gladys hadn't grabbed donuts from Conley's while she was at Family Dollar. Donuts sounded good right now. I settled for a cheesy bagel and brought along some crackers and spinach dip to the living room.

Gladys had everything all set up and was standing at the white board, ready for action. "Ok, let's get started. What do we know for sure? Should we write down that Chad was a jerk and probably had more than one person wishing he was dead?"

"I think we can save a Post-it and leave that as an unwritten fact. Let's start with who was there at the office that night, besides me and Chad. I think that has to be the list of potential murderers. Since there weren't any other vehicles seen on the surveillance tape, let's assume for now that it has to be one of those five. We know who the vehicles belong to now. Sara, Cindy, Gary, Mable (she was the cleaning lady) and Dexter Baker. Now what do we know about each one? I think we can eliminate the cleaning lady. She was the one that found Chad and reported it. She was apparently very shaken up and she didn't have any motive. That just leaves us the other four."

Gladys had made sticky notes for each of the suspects and marked a big X across Mable's name. She had notes for me and Chad as well. She had added 'jerk' to his label and put an X on mine too. "Ok, so let's not eliminate anyone else yet. Let's see what we know about them and see if we have any ideas on motive or any clues at all. Let's do them alphabetically. What do we know about Cindy, other than she was a Southern belle slut having an affair with Chad?" She jotted 'slut' on a note and stuck it up under Cindy.

"Well, she was very motivated to climb the corporate ladder and willing to do anything to get the partners attention. She was capable, maybe. I really have my doubts on that. She seemed too dainty to have the strength to actually stab Chad. I don't understand what her motive would have been either. I'm sure she was not jealous. I don't think she could care less about me. I want to believe it was her but I just can't picture it."

"Ok, she doesn't have much going for her except that we hate her. Maybe her motive was to take Chad's spot on the 8th floor. Maybe they only had one office available for a new partner and she wanted it really bad." Gladys wrote ambitious and ruthless on separate notes and stuck them up there. She wrote dainty with a question mark on a note and added it to the mix. "Not very much to go on. How about this Dexter kid. What's his story?"

"After yesterday, I am beginning to wonder. I got really bad vibes off him. I'd met him at the Christmas party and didn't get the same vibes then. Didn't pay much attention to him. I would have said he was a bit nerdy without enough gumption to commit murder. Now, he had a negative edge to him. Him meeting up with that Eddie guy is very strange. If he is really a bad guy what would Dexter be doing with him? It doesn't seem like it could have anything to do with Chad but maybe stick a note up there that he knows Eddie. Dexter certainly was physically capable of killing Chad but I'm not sure what his motive would be. He has years before he would ever be seriously considered for partnership in the firm." Gladys was sticking up notes with edgy, bad vibes, knows Eddie, a big question mark by motive.

"Ok, so Dexter is a bit unknown. What about Gary? How would you sum him up?"

"Mild mannered, super nice guy. He was hired six months before Chad and was his best friend there. He got married a couple years ago and has a six month old child. His wife Mindy has decided to stay home and raise the family. Gary had joked at the Christmas party how their lives had changed since the baby came along. Not getting much sleep and he insinuated it had been awhile since they had had sex. Chad had been crude and said something about being glad we weren't ever going to have kids. He had flashed his Rolex and said something about wanting to be able to afford his favorite things too. Gary had seemed to laugh it off saying it was getting harder and harder to keep up with the Joneses. Gary is just trying to make enough for his growing family to live in Ada. He was a football player in college and has kept in shape so definitely would be physically able but I cannot imagine him being mean enough. Only motive would be taking Chad's slot as next in line to make partner."

"Maybe Gary cared more about keeping up with Chad than you thought. Maybe he thought since he was hired first he should have been next in line for promotion, how did Chad leapfrog him anyway? Maybe Gary had something festering that could make him mean. Could he have a mean streak you never saw? Like Dexter? Maybe he was pretty desperate to make enough money to support his lifestyle. That can be pretty hard these days on one income." Gladys stuck up notes saying strong enough, motive $$, and maybe Dr. Jekyll.

"Gary was just a big old teddy bear but you are right. Maybe he was desperate. And I guess there could be a small chance that he has a side I've never seen. I'm not sure this is getting us anywhere if we keep finding everyone a potential suspect. Let's move on to Sara. It wouldn't make much sense to keep her in the running since she was attacked too. She is certainly physically capable but I don't know that she would have any motive."

"Other than Chad was a jerk and she had to put up with him. That might push anyone over the edge. Heck, it would push me over the edge." Gladys paused, thinking. "What was Sara attacked with?"

I hesitated. What was it that LuAnn had said about her wounds? "I'm pretty sure LuAnn said it was the same scissors that killed Chad."

Gladys' eyes sparkled, "how could that be if the scissors were found stuck in Chad's chest? If Chad was still sitting in his chair, he must have been killed before he had a chance to stand up and defend himself. Even as big a jerk as he was he wouldn't have sat there watching Sara get attacked without standing up and doing something. You think the killer would kill Chad, defend himself against Sara trying to save Chad then stick the scissors back into Chad? That just doesn't make sense."

"Wait, LuAnn also said that Sara's wounds were made to look self-inflicted. What if they really were? But why would she have done that? And if she was wounded first, could she have still had the strength to kill Chad? Would someone else come in and use the scissors on Chad?"

"Hold the phone. You say Sara had self-inflicted wounds? What do you know about Sara?"

"Well, not a lot really. She's from Australia, a bit of a loner. Only been here a couple of years though so not a big network of friends. She's gay, no partner but according to office rumors in love with someone she cannot have and gets moody about it. She has a body-building hobby. That's about all I know. Maybe she was lonely at Christmas and had a breakdown in Chad's office and the killer came in before Chad could call 911. Maybe the murderer just acted on impulse and stabbed him before either of them had time to think."

"So even following all of your maybes, I think there is less of a chance but still a slim possibility that Sara is still a suspect. That means any of the four could have done it."

"Cindy would have had to come back to his office, assuming she was the one under his desk when I was there. She could have forgotten something. Maybe. What would drive her to murder? And could she? Especially having to step over Sara to get to him. I just can't see it happening."

"Heck, hard to imagine any of this being real but weird bad stuff happens all the time. Don't you ever listen to

My Favorite Murder podcast? Pretty unbelievable stuff happening all the time."

I didn't have time to respond. My phone was ringing. LuAnn was calling to give me an update on her morning. I glanced at the clock. It was almost noon. "Lu, what's up? I'm putting you on speakerphone because I have Gladys here with me. We are trying to wade through some of the suspects. How did your morning go? Learn anything new?"

"As a matter of fact, yes. It was a very productive morning. I started early with breakfast with Detective Rodriquez. He did share that they had a positive ID on the prints from Chad's office. The scissors had been wiped clean (well at least the parts sticking out of Chad's body). Only prints or DNA on the blades were Sara's and Chad's. They not only found your prints on the door, there were also Sara's, Chad's, Cindy's and Mable's prints on the door. But he did say it could have been pushed open without making prints. They did eliminate Mable as a suspect. The door was closed when she arrived to clean it and she was in such shock they are convinced she didn't have anything to do with his murder.

"They also found Cindy's DNA and prints on the chair and under the desk. I guess you had already figured that out though. He also admitted they had a video of Cindy walking past the elevator towards Chad's office 15 minutes before you arrived and then her leaving a half hour after you left. She admitted to the police she was having an affair but swears Chad was fine when she left his office.

"They also have video of Gary walking towards Chad's office. He paused, glanced toward the camera and then abruptly turned around and went back the way he came. Rodriequez admitted there was something off about the move. Gary's explanation was he simply forgot something at his desk and he went back to get it. He says when he got back to his desk he was interrupted and never got back to going to see Chad. He can't seem to remember what he was interrupted with. Cops aren't buying it at all and he is supposed to go downtown tomorrow for a lie detector test. They are especially curious because apparently Gary's prints are the only ones besides Chad's on the mysterious big case file on Chad's desk. They still haven't figured out what E.H. stands for but they think it was important. Buzz in the office is Gary's sweatin' bullets. Detective Rodriequez admitted to me they consider him a flight risk and have him under surveillance. They don't have enough to haul him in and charge him but if he fails the lie detector, then they might.

"Nothing conclusive to clear you but at least there is a glimmer of doubt. They are hoping with some time the killer will crack or slip up and do something to tip his hand. Keep your fingers crossed."

"Time?! Are they crazy?? I don't want to be sitting in the lock up while they wait for the real killer to crack. I just can't stand to think about it, Lu. It just means Luke will be taking me back to GR soon. I know Hunter is supposed to meet us at the jail and I won't actually have to spend the night there. But if I do, I seriously do not know what I am going to do."

"Stop worrying. One day at a time. Gotta have faith sis. I have to scoot but you and Gladys keep working on the puzzle pieces and we can chat later."

I started to protest some more but LuAnn cut me off, "I know, I know. Hunter will not let you down. You are not going to have to stay in jail. Trust me. Oh wait, I forgot to tell you the other news; I did meet Sara's pysch nurse. We could both be fired for our discussion so not sure there is anything we can really do with the info. Sara will need to talk to the police. They are trying to convince her it will be ok. She wasn't attacked by the killer. She tried to kill herself. Apparently, she went into Chad's office after Cindy left and yelled at him about not deserving you. He laughed at her and she fled back to her desk. She went into a blind rage and picked up the scissors and went back into his office. She told him she despised him and couldn't stand it anymore. She slit her wrists and then fainted. Med team thinks she hit her head when she fell and it really wasn't Chad's killer that did it to her."

"Actually, Gladys and I had just figured that out."

"Wait. What? How?"

"Well if the scissors did all the wounds and they were stuck in Chad when he was found; Sara's injuries had to have occurred first. But if she was attacked first Chad wouldn't have been still sitting in his chair. There had to have been someone that came in after she fell and before Chad got up."

"I need to get back with Rodriquez. If you two can figure it out, his team should be able to put two and two together faster. I also want to try and talk to Sara. I think if she knows you are going down for Chad's murder, she will explain he was alive for at least an hour after you left. She has got to tell Rodriguez she saw Chad alive after you left. It still doesn't explain who killed Chad but you should be cleared. I will call you back later."

She hung up and Gladys and I got busy adding a few notes to our suspect board. We put an X through Sara's name eliminating her. We added a note about Gary's fingerprints on the EH file and one with just a big question mark under him. What was up with Gary?

It was after 3 o'clock and I had to get ready for my mission helping Luke. I still hadn't told him about seeing Eddie yesterday. Maybe best that I didn't tell him right now. Not like it mattered to his case.

Gladys was ready to take a break anyway so it was easy to bustle her out of there to go home and take a nap. I think she was having dinner with Murray and wanted to be refreshed and ready. It was cute how he made her eyes light up.

LuAnn facetimed me just as I was getting ready to head downstairs to go. She picked up on my ninja outfit right away. "What in the world kind of fashion statement is that? Have you gone into mourning? You are gonna want to change once you hear my good news."

"Hey Lu, I've got to scoot. Luke needs my help so I have got to get going."

LuAnn smirked and raised her eyebrows up and down at me, "Help? Luke? Hopefully you two are hitting it off and it is something romantic. Though it is sort of hard to imagine; you're definitely not going to make any sexy points in that outfit. OMG! Have you two reached the kinky stage already!/!"

"No, get your mind out of the gutter. I'll tell you about it later. Bye." I hung up before she could say anything more. I ran over to the Palmer's to catch my ride.

CHAPTER 20

LUKE DROVE ME TO THE INN. Decided it was best not to leave Hank the Tank out there in case Charlie happened to notice and wondered who he belonged to. We pulled in right at four o'clock and found Joey and his wife Penny there getting ready for the evening diners. They were both about 60 and both still in great shape. Joey was tall, very solidly built with salt and pepper hair. He could have been a left tackle or bouncer back in the day instead of a retired state trooper. Penny was Korean, jet black hair pulled back in a tight bun. She was petite and muscular and looked like she could have been a gymnast. She was a retired deputy. Luke had filled me in on their story on the way to the Inn. "Penny met Joey when she was assigned to a case that the state police had stepped in to take over from the county sheriff department. County boys were furious to have their toes stepped on and were still getting used to having a very competent female on the force. Penny and Joey surprised everyone by hitting it off, right off the bat.

It never dawned on all the great detectives that they had fallen in love the first time they met. Penny solved the case and they have been together ever since. They retired together and bought the Inn looking forward to the peace and quiet of the little lake up North. They make a great team. They really improved the place and have a good business going. They have been really helpful in solving some of the petty crimes in the area too. Not many people know they are retired law enforcement.

They knew that crime was everywhere but they never thought they would be so actively involved in trying to shut down the latest surge in the drug cartel right here in Northern Michigan. This cartel was particularly nasty. They were into a little bit of everything; drugs, prostitution, selling illegal arms to the various militia groups around the country, human trafficking. The dregs of society."

Joey let us in then relocked the doors just in case any senior citizens tried to get a jump on the happy hour specials. Penny showed me the space they had prepared for me. She had cleaned out the shelf and even put in a yoga mat and a little pillow for me. Downright cozy. I got situated and saw Luke on his knees checking out my resting spot for the next ten hours. His face looked troubled. I tried to reassure him, "I'll be completely fine. I have LuAnn's Kindle and enough to read and do that time will fly by. No worries. Really. I got this."

Luke smiled and leaned in and kissed me, "I'll be back by seven o'clock. If anything happens in the meantime, Joey and Penny are here to look out for you." With that he hopped up and told Joey he would be back.

I lay there stunned for a few minutes. Maybe there could be something there. Maybe Luke actually liked me.

I smiled, happy to know that what I was feeling wasn't just me. Hopefully I could help him get this case wrapped up, get my name cleared and then maybe we could work on having some kind of normal relationship. My heart fluttered and I felt my cheeks blushing. I mentally slapped myself upside the head. I didn't want to spend too much time wishful thinking, definitely didn't want to jinx anything by way of over thinking it if there was something real going on between Luke and I. I sighed quietly and opened up the Kindle and buried my head in a book.

It was hard to concentrate once business started picking up. Surprised how much I could hear from my vantage point there under the bar. Most of the patrons went past the bar into the dining area. Even with all the snow the view was magnificent with picture windows facing the lake. It looked like a winter wonderland dotted with dark green pines.

A few people sat at the bar. One guy that sounded like he had been enjoying a few drinks before he got here, sat down right above my head. Penny greeted him, "Hey Sid, how's it going? Did you drive here? You don't look like you are steady enough to be behind the wheel of a car. Roads are just getting cleared and there are still some rough patches to get through."

"I'm fine Penny, I''m fine. I drove the snowmobile over. I just wanted to get a bite to eat. I've only had liquid nourishment today and I'll be better if I get something in me to soak it up."

"You do know Sid that operating any vehicle while intoxicated is illegal don't you? I can't let you drive your rig home. I will get some food into you and then I will have Jimmy run you home. He can take a break from clearing tables long enough to get you home safely. We will get your sled home to you tomorrow morning."

Sid started eating peanuts spitting out pieces while he chomped away. I knew because I could see pieces flying over the bar and hitting the floor behind the bar. Gross. I couldn't see him but I had a good mental picture in my mind. Based on his gravelly voice, it sounded like he was a pack a day smoker and had been drinking most of the day. If I had to guess, I'd say he had a scruffy beard, tattered flannel shirt over even more tattered jeans. The way his boots had jangled when he walked in it sounded like he wore the old style big black boots with buckles undone. The kind like the kid in The Christmas Story wore.

Sid grumbled a bit while giving Penny his order, "you are worse than an old mother hen you know that Penny? Where's Joe? Have him look at me, he'll tell you. I am fine. Do you want me to walk a straight line or somethin'? Just bring me a beer while I wait for my food. We can figure out how I get home after I eat." He'd spit peanuts with every word. I couldn't wait to see what came flying out of his mouth while he ate his dinner. He shouted for Penny to hurry up with his beer.

I heard her set a glass down in front of him and walk away. I was a little surprised she would serve him alcohol if he was already drunk. Next thing I knew Sid was shrieking and spewing pop all over. "What in hell is this?! Pop? I said I wanted a beer. Not this sweet crap!" And then he threw the drink down on the floor. Right beside my head. The plastic cup bounced sloshing the last of its contents onto my shelf. The dark liquid splashed everywhere. It slowly dripped off the shelf above my head. I could feel it on the side of my face. Terrific. Now I could add lying in sticky pop syrup for hours on end off my bucket list.

Sid continued to sound off and tossed the little cup of

mustard and ketchup over the counter to add an exclamation point to his tirade. Each cup was perfectly projected to bounce up in my face. Are you friggin' kidding me right now Sid?! I lay there helpless. One big condiment mess. Joey came out to usher Sid out. He was going to have someone drive him home. "Come on Sid, let's go. I have made your order to go for you. You can eat it after I get you home." It sounded like Joey picked Sid up by the scruff of his neck as he led him out the door. "Jimmy is going to take a break from busing tables just for you and take you home. I'll get your sled to you tomorrow after you've had a chance to sober up and sleep this off."

Penny was trying to clean up the mess, whispering she was so sorry to me. She slipped me a wet wash rag so I could wipe off my face. Hopefully that would be the extent of my thrills for the evening. I tried focusing on my book. Nothing I could do about my matted down hair except push my bangs out of my eyes.

Luke showed up early. I knew he was there as soon as he walked in. It was almost like there was a change in air pressure or something. I could smell the subtle hint of his body wash as he sat down at the bar. His warm sexy scent and just having him near made me shiver. I took a deep breath as quietly as I could and felt the calm spread through me. I started to get teary eyed when I heard him whisper, "are you ok down there?" It was probably good there was no way I could actually answer him. I would have choked on my tears.

Joey stopped by at the end of the counter to say hello and ask Luke what he was having tonight. Luke said, "Just give me a 7&7." I knew it would be a virgin one. Luke had already explained to me that he and Joey had worked it out before. Luke didn't actually drink alcohol while he was here since he is on duty. Joey had filled a couple of whiskey decanters with decoy beverages, iced tea in one and thinned down Amish maple syrup in the other. He used that to fill Luke's drinks. Guessing a 7&7 was 7-Up and maple syrup. Might have to try it sometime.

Joey set down Luke's drink and went to help another customer. I heard Luke whisper to me again, "Lacey I know you can't talk but please just give me a little knock if you are ok. Knock twice if you need anything. I can't stand having you down there not knowing if you are ok or not."

I tapped once on the shelf fighting back tears. Choked me up that Luke cared about me. It took all my willpower to not fall off the shelf and scramble around into Luke's arms. I wished we had met under different circumstances. Just maybe, we could have had a real relationship instead of him being my captor and having to turn me into the jail tomorrow.

I heard Luke greet Charlie, "Hey Charlie, grab a stool. What's happenin' ?" Luke sounded a little off but that might be tension holding himself back from choking the crap out of Charlie for what he had done to Gladys. Luke had to have nerves of steel to sit next to him and not throw cuffs on him. I gave a silent prayer that our little sting operation worked so Luke could finally take care of Charlie for good.

Charlie mumbled a reply. I couldn't quite make it out. Luke was trying to cajole him, "things can't be that bad Charlie. Tomorrow is New Year's eve. Get to ring in a new year. That's always exciting. Got any big plans?"

Joey interrupted, checking to see if Charlie wanted his usual Pabst. Charlie grumbled, "of course I do and keep 'em comin'"". He turned to Luke and answered, "I sure hope I have a fantastic New Year's. Been plannin' on it for months. It has been a hellava year and I am due for a fresh start that's for damn sure."

Joey brought Charlie his drink. Pabst in a frosted mug. With a shot of vodka added. Charlie didn't know about the extra shot. Luke had told me of their plan to spike Charlie's drinks to help speed up his inebriation. Apparently Charlie talked even more once he reached his tipping point. I could hear Charlie chug the beer. "Ah, that tastes great Joey. Go ahead and pour me another. I'll finish this by the time you get back here with it."

Luke laughed, "man, you must be thirsty. Whatcha been doin' to work up such a thirst? Catching lots of fish? More than the limit?"

Charlie's laugh sounded almost sinister. "I've been catching lots, that's for sure. Gonna have to get me another freezer if I keep this up."

"What are you stockpiling for?"

"This latest armageddon snow is just the tip of the iceberg man. I wanna be ready in case I need to lay low for a few months. You never know when you might have to. It could be the end of the world as we know it. I've been preparing for it for a long time. Dude, it's best to be uber-prepared, I always say."

"Good to know. If I get hungry I might stop by for a visit." Luke tried to make his chuckle sound lighthearted. I thought it sounded off. I could just picture Luke trying to maintain an interested look on his face. Charlie was clearly a nut job.

"No offense man but every man for himself. You need to take care of yourself. Say man, what were you doing with those freakin' women the other day? I saw you drive by with both of them. Didn't see the old biddy when you left the hardware store though. How can you stand being around those bitches?"

Luke sighed a little to give himself time to keep his cool again. "Oh that, they asked me for a ride to the store. Afraid to try driving there themselves cause they weren't sure of the roads. The old lady had taken a tumble and they were afraid of her falling again. They are both a little crazy but really aren't so bad if you ignore them mostly. Luckily I only come up once in a blue moon to visit grandpa so I don't have to put up with them really. I was just being neighborly."

Charlie grunted, "screw that. I hope I never see either of those two witches again. The old bitch fell did she? Too bad she didn't break her neck. Those bitches are a pain in my ass. Always snooping around. What I do is none of their damn business. I hate nosy people." He must have been waving his arms around because all of a sudden I heard his mug topple over and the rest of his beer came dribbling over the bar and onto my shelf. Nice. Real nice.

What a prick. I recognized Joey's black boots when he brought Charlie his second beer and mopped up the mess Charlie had made. He paused, "Speaking of nosey, I see Officer James O'Reilly's pulled into the lot. Hopefully neither of you boys have any warrants out for your arrest or any outstanding parking tickets. I'd hate to have him have to haul you in just before his quittin' time. Nothin' makes a cop crankier than having to deal with arrest paperwork when he should be home with his honey."

I heard Luke's stool scrape back. "I gotta hit the head. Watch my spot Charlie, I'll be right back." Luke moved off to the restroom while Charlie sucked down his second beer with just a few gulps.

Joey greeted O'Reilly and shot the breeze about the road conditions while he rang up his order. He must have called it in because Penny was already carrying it out before Joey had given him his change. I could hear O'Reilly's Sam Browne squeak from all the equipment he had loaded on it as he shifted his weight back and forth on his feet. His voice was a deep baritone, "Charlie Hooper, what are you doing these days? Up to any good?"

Charlie's response was unintelligible from my perch on the shelf. O'Reilly didn't seem perturbed, "just keep yourself out of trouble Charlie. See you around Joey, Penny."

CHAPTER 21

I COULD HEAR THE BELL ON THE door ding as Officer O'Reilly left the restaurant. Joey and Penny went back into the kitchen leaving me alone with Charlie right above me. My butt was starting to ache, just as Charlie started sputtering. I don't think he was talking to anyone in particular just himself and just loud enough for me to hear, "Damn cops. I hate the bastards. Always think they are better than everyone else. Always harassing me. I ain't done nothin' wrong. Well not much. Nothin' they need to bother me 'bout anyways. I hate those cocksuckers. They are always itchin' to make my life miserable. Always driving by to do a check on all the fancy ass rich people's empty cottages. Damn people don't need half the shit they cart up here and they ain't gonna miss the few things I borrow to make my life a little more comfortable. I am actually doing a good thing, putting items to good use instead of letting them rust and collect dust in their la-te-da vacation homes. Spoiled bunch of hypocrites. Bastards. Come up here to get back to nature with three, four, five damn

TVs."

Luke came back from the restroom and could see Charlie was upset. "Hey, Charlie, looks like we need another round. Whaddaya say?"

Charlie growled, "make it a double. I gotta get the bad taste of cop out of my mouth."

"What happened? O'Reilly ticket you or something?"

"Nah, bastard just bugs me, that's all. He don't scare me none."

They sat drinking and watching the game. College football bowl games, the universal male bonding moment. Charlie was slurring his words by the time he finished his third beer. "Man, this is good beer Joey. It packs a nice punch. Must be 'cause it is on draft. Way better than I get in the cans I usually buy. I better go relieve myself if I'm gonna drink anymore."

Charlie staggered off to the bathroom. Joey came over closer and Luke whispered, "thanks for the heads up on O'Reilly. He would have blown my cover for sure. You think Charlie is going to spill anything?"

I cringed thinking of the pop and beer splashing in my face before I remembered he meant Charlie spilling any details about the transfer that was supposed to take place soon. Joey wiped the bar and nodded to a couple that was leaving. He waited until he heard the bell on the door before responding. "I think so. He seems easily agitated tonight. I'll send Penny over with another double shot round. She can usually get a rise out of him and might get him going."

They both went back to staring at the game as Charlie came back to his stool. Joey walked into the kitchen and Penny came out with another round of drinks, some fresh bread and an order of shrimp cocktail for both Luke and

Charlie. "Here you go, on the house. Had a cancellation on this order and no sense having it go to waste. You two could use something to sop up all that booze you've been guzzling. So Charlie, got a hot date planned for New Year's eve?"

Charlie was so shocked by Penny's question he choked on his beer. The gulp he was taking flew across the bar. Luke started slapping Charlie on his back. "Whoa, Charlie, take it easy. You ok?" Charlie just sputtered and coughed. Penny calmly took to wiping up the mess. Casually dropping a dry towel on my shelf so I could wipe up the few beer drops that had made their way down to me.

Luke's phone rang and he went out to the small vestibule to take the call. Penny finished wiping up and left Charlie to recover. She had no sooner got into the kitchen when Charlie started. "Damn straight I've got a hot date bitch. I'm gonna have the best three-way ever. Well, if Eddie will let me have her for a night before we trade. Yeah, I'm gonna ring in the new year big alright. I'm sure Eddie will let me try the merchandise first. I'll tell him I gotta sample it before we seal the deal. I'll give that worthless piece I've got to him after I show her what she's missing by being such a whiny bitch. Eddie will be thankful if I teach her a lesson. Yeah. It's gonna be some hot date that's for sure."

I lay there stunned. What was he talking about? Did he actually have a girl in his cabin that he was planning on trading with Eddie? What did that have to do with the bloody tarps he had been dragging down to the lake? What was this lunatic up to?

Charlie drank in silence for a little bit while I lay on my stealthy shelf chewing my bottom lip trying to put all the pieces of his bizarre comments and behavior together. Penny poked her head out of the kitchen, "Can I get you anything else Charlie? More cocktail sauce?" Charlie picked up the half empty container and went to hand it back to Penny even though she was over ten feet away. He misjudged the distance in his drunken state and the container fell to the floor right by my head. The small crash of the container made me jump and bump my head on the shelf. I froze. Oh my gosh, what if Charlie heard me?

Penny came running out as Charlie jumped up leaning over the counter. "Whoa, what happened down there? Sounded bad."

As Charlie tried to peer over the counter, Penny was shooing him back onto his stool. "It's fine Charlie. I got it. No harm done." Easy for her to say. I now had red cocktail sauce smeared across my face and into my hair along with the sticky pop, mustard and ketchup from earlier. The smell of horseradish was going to make me gag. Wouldn't that be perfect if I added throw up to the mix? Penny wiped up the mess and gave Charlie a fresh side of sauce and went back to the kitchen.

Charlie started yammering again the second she cleared the door. "I'll tell ya whatcha can get for me. Bend that ass over the bar and I'll show you a real man. Like to take a poke at that. I love me a good piece of Asian ass. You're too old to keep though. I need a nice young piece of ass I can have all to myself for a while. I don't want your old sloppy seconds. Once Eddie brings me my new girl, I'll be all set. Ring in the new year with a new wife that actually knows how to behave and keep me satisfied. Got enough venison stocked now so I can stay out of sight for months. Gonna be perfect. Just me and her all day long. Gonna be perfect."

I heard Charlie groan and I would have sworn I heard him unzip his pants. No way. Right there at the bar? Eeewww. This guy is so gross. I could tell from his moans he was doing something. I did not want to listen and get any more mental images. I plugged my ears and tried holding my breath to help dull the sounds.

"Whoa, Charlie! What in hell are you doing man??" Thankfully Luke walked back in and I could breathe again. "Put that thing away. Joey's gonna throw your ass outta here. Hell he will throw you all the way back to your place. What's going on?"

Charlie zipped himself back in, "oh, sorry dude. I forgot where I was for a minute. I just got thinking and got carried away. You know how it is."

"You got a girlfriend Charlie? Who are you thinking about that made you into a horn-dog right here at the bar? Must be someone special."

"Oh yeah, she's special alright."

"You should have brought her here with you. I would like to meet her."

I could feel Charlie turn cold all the way down where I was. He went completely silent. Luke sensed he'd crossed a line too and started trying to backtrack. "Hey, I didn't mean anything by it Charlie. Really. Don't take offense."

Charlie slammed his fists down on the bar rattling all the glasses. It made me jump and bump my head again but fortunately in the commotion no one seemed to notice. Charlie scraped his stool back roughly and said in a very cold, steely voice, "don't be getting any ideas pretty boy. You ain't gonna steal my girl. She's all mine and I ain't sharin' even if it is just for looking." Charlie hollered for Joey. "I'm leavin'. I'll settle up with you later."

Joey came around the corner of the bar, pausing as he too sensed the increased tension in the air. "No problem Charlie. You ok to make it home?"

"Yeah, I rode the sled. I'll go home back across the lake and stay off the roads mostly. I'll be fine." I heard the doorbell ping and he was gone.

I stayed frozen in place. Afraid to come out because I wasn't sure how many customers were still there. Joey must have read my mind because I heard him whisper, "Hang tight Lacey. Only one table left to clear out and we are sending staff home. We'll close up early and get you off that shelf shortly." To Luke, he bluntly asked, "What the hell just happened here? What did you do to piss Charlie off?"

"I have no idea. I stayed out in the lobby for a bit, thanks for the call diversion by the way, worked great, I think. Anyway, I came back in and Charlie had his pecker in his hand and was just about ready to go to town. So I guess maybe that coulda made him pretty mad. He seemed to really get pissed though when I said I'd like to meet his girl. He just lost it then."

"Back up, Charlie was going to whack himself off right here at the bar?!? What the hell! And Charlie has a girl? You sure you heard that right? He hasn't had a girl since his mail order bride ran off on him last summer. Hang on a sec and let me get Jimmy and Mandy out of here. I'll be right back."

Joey went to tend to the last customers and let his staff of two go home for the evening. He and Penny would take care of cleaning up. After locking the door and flipping the closed sign on, Joey came back behind the bar and reached down to give me a hand up. I was stiff from lying there so long. I must have looked a fright. Luke's eyes couldn't hide his mirth and I could tell he was choking back a laugh. I stood up tall and put my hands on my hips. "What? Do not even think about laughing at me right now buddy."

Luke held his hands up in surrender, "nothing, really. I just didn't realize you were in such a hazard zone down there."

I looked down. It was hard to see it all completely on my black attire but the mustard looked almost neon. The red blotches on my hands were either the ketchup or the cocktail sauce. I turned to look into the mirror behind the bottles on the bar and almost gasped in horror. My hair was stiff and plastered in a strange configuration from all the sticky ingredients. Good grief. I looked like a freak show. I tried to ignore it. "Listen, Charlie does have a girl. She is what he plans to trade with Eddie. He was ranting about having a threesome once he got the other girl from Eddie. If Eddie will let him have them both for a night. He got all agitated after Penny asked him if he had a hot date for New Year's eve."

I told them everything I had heard Charlie say. Even the lewd comments about Penny because I figured she was safer if she knew. I shuddered when I was done recounting his mini-tirades. Not gonna lie. Charlie scared me. Scared me a lot. I started shaking and couldn't stop.

Luke came around the bar and took me in his arms. Calmly telling me to take big, deep breaths. Holding me and ignoring the sticky mess that I was. I gulped in air and slowly felt my panic subsiding. I sighed. Suddenly I was completely exhausted. I just wanted to go home. Well to LuAnn's, and take a long hot shower. I needed to wash the memory of Charlie off of me. Along with the pop, beer, mustard, ketchup and cocktail sauce.

Luke thanked Penny and Joey and led me out the kitchen entrance. He had moved his truck around back when he took his fake call earlier. He wanted to be sure no one saw me leaving. His caring and protective nature towards me made my eyes well up. I'd better get home quick. I was going to be a basket case soon.

Linda Shoaf

CHAPTER 22

LUKE HELPED ME INTO THE HOUSE and told me to lock up. He was going to go check on a couple things and be back shortly. I was actually relieved. I needed to be alone for a little bit. I didn't want to worry he could hear me if I started sobbing in the shower.

The shower did me wonders but I still felt completely drained. Amazing how strenuous lying on a shelf and listening could be. I was dozing off in front of the fire when Luke got back. "Are you ok?" He asked so softly and gently. I was so lucky to have him as my jailor. He genuinely cared and it warmed my heart.

"Yes, I'm much better thank you. I must say I can't recommend the Coke mousse or the mustard, ketchup and cocktail sauce face mask. No great beauty finds. Though, speaking of cocktail sauce, I am very thirsty and hungry.

We moved to the kitchen and settled into our spots at the counter. We ate fruit and guzzled bottled water by the light of the under-cabinet lighting. It gave the room a cozy feel. Luke explained his errands. "I went back to talk to Joey and I made a quick visit to the ice shanty. Pretty sure Charlie's venison stockpile has been made this week. The deer are easy pickings with all this snow. It looks like he has been slaughtering them and then dumping the evidence down his fishing hole. I'll have a warrant drawn up and call in the DNR. With any luck we will have a search warrant for the house too since the meat is likely stored there and then we can see what is really going on in there. Hopefully I can get it taken care of early tomorrow so we can get you back to GR."

I tried not to let the thought of getting back to my problems cloud the issue at hand of catching Charlie. "What about the swap with Eddie? Shouldn't you wait so you can catch him too?"

"I know but I really wanted to get you back so Hunter can get you cleared quickly so you don't have to spend New Year's eve in jail. I'm sure he will already have the skids greased but sometimes the wheels of justice turn slowly, especially on holidays."

I didn't know what to say. I just hung my head. He was right but did it really matter whether I spent a lonely New Year's eve at home or in jail? If staying a few more hours or another day helped some poor girl stuck with Eddie, any jail time I might have would be worth it. I tried explaining what I was thinking to Luke.

He smiled and told me I was amazing. He picked up his phone and dialed. Joey picked up on the first ring. "Hey, I was just going to call you. I just heard back from my informant. Eddie is headed our way tomorrow. He just heard Eddie get off the phone with Charlie. Eddie wants to make the exchange tomorrow at 3 o'clock at Charlie's place. We need the warrants and a full team in place before then. Tell Lacey great work and that if we bag Eddie tomorrow too, she gets free meals anytime."

I smiled. What a great thought. Free meals would be nice but locking up both Charlie and Eddie, that would be fantastic. Plus I would get a bonus day with Luke. Sort of. He would be busy and I'm sure I wasn't going to get to tag along but at least I'd be up here with him. Besides, I needed to do some more leg work on my own case. Another day would certainly help. Maybe Sara would talk and explain my innocence. Maybe Lu will have more info from the police investigation. Speaking of Lu, I'd better call her and explain what was going on up here. It wasn't even 11:30 yet. She's probably still up watching the news. I went off to call LuAnn while Luke went up to take a shower himself.

I didn't even hear the phone ring on her end but Lu answered the phone in a panic, "Are you ok? What is wrong? Do you know what time it is??"

"Yes Lu, it's almost 11:30. I am fine. I just wanted to tell you I'll have to stay up here another day. Luke has an important case he is working and we have to stay. Besides another day and maybe my name will be cleared so I won't have to hurry back right? Have you heard anything?"

"Nothing more but Detective Rodriquez did agree to meet me in the morning. We decided to share our notes and ideas. Going to see if anything pops out at us. I also have a coffee break date with the nurse that works with the psychologist seeing Sara. Hopefully we will get to the bottom of it all tomorrow.

"That sounds great. Thanks Lu. Love you, talk to you tomorrow." I hung up feeling happier than I had in a long time. I could feel the tide shifting. Tomorrow will be a good day. I was still smiling when Luke walked in fresh from the shower. I froze. Luke was so relaxed. I'm not sure he even felt the electricity in the air. If he did, he was great at looking calm and collected. My trance was broken by the sudden buzz of the timer on the oven. Luke spun around explaining as he walked back into the kitchen, "I took the liberty of making us pizza for a late night snack. I was still starving. I hope that is ok."

"Perfect, let's eat here in the living room. Might as well be extra comfortable."

"Do you want some wine? Or do you want something stronger? You have been through a lot tonight."

"Wine is good. I'm actually feeling fine. So glad my listening was able to help. Charlie is one messed up guy. Hopefully he can get some of the help he so desperately needs."

"That's a nice thought Lacey but I'm pretty sure Charlie is too far gone. Not sure he will ever be truly well. He's had trauma all his life. His father was abusive and took a lot out on Charlie. He was an only child and took the brunt of all of his father's anger toward life. He dropped out of school and went into the Army. Stationed in Vietnam and after the war stationed in Korea he retired. Not sure what happened but he came back and lived in the U.P. until his mother passed away and left her place on the lake to him. He moved down here and has been a loner pretty much ever since."

"Pretty sad really. I hope he hasn't hurt the girl that is with him."

"Hard to say. He probably thought he was getting a deal on a new wife. Since he is trading her, she must not have worked out like he was hoping and likely will not hurt her because it would diminish her trade value. It is a sick business."

"Ok, I can't think about him anymore. Way too depressing. Can we just turn out the lights and look at the stars for a while?"

"Great idea." Luke turned off all the lights and lay down on the couch with me. We fell into a companionable silence and fell into our own thoughts. I was fighting a wave of sadness washing over me at the realization that this would be the last time I would be with him. Tomorrow it will be over. His case would be solved and I'd get transported back to the big city to deal with my own nightmare. It might not be completely awful since I should be cleared of murder. That went into the plus column. But, until the real murderer was behind bars I'd have people wondering what my role in Chad's death really was.

Luke felt the tear that had been rolling down my cheek as it hit his arm. "Lacey, Lacey what's wrong?" Thankfully, he folded me tighter in his arms before I could respond. "It's going to be ok Lacey. Trust me. You do trust me don't you?" He held me back slightly so he could see into my eyes. His kiss warmed me all through my entire body. I think I melted a little. I felt a little like Silly Putty warmed in the sun; slowly molding myself to fit perfectly up against his broad chest and into his arms. A sigh slipped from my lips and we both fell back, kissing with energy that surprised us both.

I'm not sure which one of us came up for air first. A small "whoa" escaped with one of my breaths and Luke simply murmured, "yeah". Our hands had been gently investigating each other, almost like they had minds of their own. Luke gently took my hands away from his washboard stomach and kissed them saying, "I cannot be-

lieve I am saying this Lacey but we have to slow down."
My eyes must have had a spark of hurt because he quickly
kissed me and continued, "no Lacey, not because I don't
want you. I do. Real bad. But I want it on our terms and
not when you are exhausted and vulnerable. Trust me,
once this is all over, we can pick this up again." He kissed
me again and we laid on the couch until we both drifted
off to sleep.

Linda Shoaf

CHAPTER 23

I'M NOT SURE HOW OR WHEN IT HAP-
pened but somehow I wound up back in my bed. I
woke up with a warmth and lightness in my heart
that I don't remember ever feeling. Had last night really
happened?

I was barely dressed and downstairs before the doorbell rang. Gladys bounced in in her usual exuberant style.
Leopard print yoga pants with matching leopard print
cowl neck tunic with oversized bedazzled aviators hiding
her purple eyes. Her brilliance put my simple leggings
and cowl neck sweater to shame.

"That boy sure seemed happy."

I couldn't stop the grin from popping out on my face
fast enough.

"Hey wait a minute. Luke's not beaming because
you're beaming is he? Did you two tangle the sheets last
night? Come on, spill the beans."

"No, Gladys, we did not twist the sheets. We certainly did have a connection though. Luke's too much of a
gentleman though and we didn't go past second base. He

wants to wait until we can have a real date without all this drama hanging over our heads. Did Luke fill you in on Charlie this morning?"

"Yeah, said he's going down at three and gave me strict orders to stay here with you. He even took my .44 away from me again. Said he didn't want me getting any crazy ideas. I brought over some high powered binoculars for both of us. I figure we can get set up in front of the picture window and watch the action from there. Unless you think we should get some of Harry's hunting guns out and go over and give Luke some backup. He might need us."

"No. I think Luke will have enough backup. The Feds are interested in Eddie and the cartel he represents. I'm sure they will have lots of agents here to help. Let's see if a fresh look at our suspect board gives us any more answers."

Gladys and I settled in to work. Best to keep occupied with my predicament rather than count the minutes until the cartel take down. I took off the notes on those we had eliminated and made columns for the remaining three potentials. "So, let's sum up what we have on our viable suspects. Cindy: driven, ambitious, ruthless, weak."

Gladys piped up, "don't forget sleazebag slut."

I rolled my eyes but added the additional color commentary. "Let's move on. Gary: suspicious, broke (needs money), jealous?, fingerprints on the EH file, physically capable. Dexter: ambitious, knows Eddie, bad vibe."

Gladys jumped up and started jabbing at Eddie's name under Dexter's column. "There is something going on here. What is the connection?"

It suddenly hit me. "Chad's secret, 'I'm gonna get rich quick and blow this pop stand law practice file. EH. Eddie Hawkins! I can't believe I missed making the connection before. What was Chad messed up in? Were Dexter and / or Gary mixed up in it as well?"

Gladys plopped back down in her chair. "Well, I guess this means we can eliminate the slut. But if you ask me, we should still send her a cow patty care package since she is such a piece of shit. Just sayin'."

I had to chuckle. The vision of Cindy excited to get a present and opening her gift only to get covered in cow manure would certainly be a sight to behold. "Maybe some other time Gladys. Let's just get the murderer first. Are you hungry? I'm starving. It's already after one, if we hurry we can get to Conley's before they close and get back here in time to watch Charlie's arrest."

"Sounds great. There's probably slim pickings since they sell out some days but maybe we can buy out the rest of the donuts to give to all the cops up here today. Wouldn't hurt to get on their good side. I do wanna be back in time for the take down. Nothing this exciting ever happens up here."

It was a great plan and would have probably been fine if Gladys wasn't such a spectacle in her bedazzled glasses. They drew more stares than her blackeyes would have. I'd left her in Hank when I ran in to grab donuts and as I climbed back in, Gladys says, "I think they noticed me."

"Really? You think so? Pretty hard not to miss you in that get up. Who noticed you?"

Gladys huffed a little. "I was just sitting here minding my own business and I heard these two guys talking in the car that you parked next to. I listened without looking at them for a little bit. They were talking about the big boss getting up here early cause he was supposed to meet up with his new lawyer to talk before the deal. I turned to look who they were and they burst out laughing and peeled out. Not sure what that was all about."

"Oh no! Early! We have got to get back and warn Luke!"

It didn't take long to drive back but as we pulled up to Lake Drive, we had to slow down as a car ahead of us was turning onto Lake Drive too. There was a car waiting to turn left onto it too. Awful lot of traffic for this road. I looked into the car waiting to turn left. The driver was a very mean looking Mexican with slits for eyes. He glanced at Gladys and I could see his gold teeth when he smiled. It was more of a sneer but he started pointing and spoke over his shoulder as if he was telling someone in the back to look at the goofy old lady.

Gladys noticed and scooted up in the seat to peer out the windshield. She started waving and shouting, "that's them! That's them!" She started hitting me wanting me to speed up and ram the car in front of us.

The car that had turned right onto the road before us went past the road to the cottage and didn't seem to be noticing what was going on behind them. I tried to calmly make my right turn and get to the cottage without flooring it. Gladys was bouncing up and down on the seat and kept checking behind us to make sure they were still coming. The driver certainly looked like a bad guy. If it was Eddie in the car, he was over an hour early. And he wasn't alone. I could see the driver talking over his shoulder and then pick up his phone.

I was starting to panic. What if they realized we were on to them and alerted Charlie? I had to call Luke and warn him fast. I pulled into LuAnn's garage and watched the black Land Rover go by as the door closed. I was calling Luke praying he was somewhere where he could answer. He picked up on the first ring with a sharp, "What!"

I was breathing so hard and so fast I could hardly get any words out. "Bad guys coming, we got donuts, met bad guys on the road. They saw us...."

Luke whispered, "Lacey slow down. What are you trying to tell me?"

Exasperated, Gladys grabbed the phone. "Black Land Rover headed your way. ETA two minutes or less. They may have gotten suspicious when we looked at them. They were calling someone. Be ready and be careful." She hung up and handed me back my phone. Now let's hurry up and see if we can tell what is going on. Don't forget to bring in the donuts."

I groaned and grabbed the donuts. My stomach was churning but maybe a maple glazed donut or two would settle my nerves. Or make me throw up faster. I got into the house to see Gladys plastered up against the front window with her ginormous binoculars saying, "I can see a couple of feds fake fishing down on the ice. Fools. Nobody goes out there without a shanty. They stick out like a sore thumb. If there are more of them, at least they are better hidden. I can't see Luke. I think I can see the car that was in front of us parked by Watson's place. It is all boarded up so they can tell no one is there. I gotta pee."

Gladys headed to the bathroom while I took up her post at the window. I took up my binoculars and scanned across the lake. I could see the Rover drive by Charlie's without even pausing. It was going to take a while for it to come back. No place to turn around. I saw movement at Charlie's door and saw him peek out. He looked both ways then straight across the lake straight at me. I ducked. Not that he could see me but it scared me. By the time I peeked back up he was gone. I couldn't see him. He must have gone back inside. I continued to scan the area and saw the guys on the lake and the car parked at Watson's place. Nothing was moving out there. It was eerie and more than a little nerve racking.

Gladys opened the bathroom door asking, "do you have any of that white sunscreen stuff that you usually put on your nose to keep it from burning? Oh nevermind, found some here in the cupboard." She walked out and was smearing it on her lips.

I had to do a head slap. Gladys stood there all dressed in white. White winter hat, with white Cuddle Duds top and pants. Completed with white marshmallow coat and white moon boots and a white fanny pack. "Gladys, what in the world do you think you are doing?"

"I am covering up the Hot Mama Cherry Red lipstick. I tried rubbing it off but it has real staying power. Handy for romantic moments but a killer when you want to make sure you blend in and don't want anyone noticing you."

I slapped myself on the head again. Is she serious right now? "Blend in where?"

"I'm just going to pop out for a quick second and see if I can get a better look at what is going on. I will blend right in with all the snow banks and no one will ever know I am even there."

"Oh hell no. You are not going out there right now!"

Gladys was out the door before I could finish telling her no. I slapped myself on the head a few more times. I ran to the door to peek out but of course could not see her anywhere. I ran back to get my binoculars and ran upstairs to see if I could spot her out one of the side windows. Maybe up high would give me a better vantage point. I frantically looked at all the neighbors' houses I could see between LuAnn's and Charlie's. I finally spotted her about 50 yards behind the car from Conley's that was parked at the Watson's. She was crawling like one of the green army men on the ground up to the car. My phone rang and I had a mini-heart attack. I snatched it up and didn't even say hello and I heard Luke whisper screaming at me. "Tell me that is not Gladys doing G.I. Joe maneuvers behind the tan Volvo at the Watson house. What in God's name is she doing? Is she armed? Does she have any idea how dangerous this is? I thought you had control of her. What is going on?"

"If you would take a breath for a sec please. First of all control Gladys? Are you kidding me? Good luck with that. I had no idea she was prepped and ready wearing her winter white snow suit under her leopard outfit today. She pulled a fast one on me. I don't think she is armed but I didn't do a body search on her. She said you had her .44 so she's probably not. I only saw shotguns that Earl had over there and we would notice one if she was packing one of those. Pretty sure she doesn't have a clue on the danger. She's just trying to help. We figured out Dexter knows Eddie and I'm sure she is just trying to see if she hears any more that might give us some clues."

"Whoa, hold up mam. What did you say? Dexter knows Eddie? Who in hell is Dexter and what clues? What does any of whoever Dexter is have to do with what is going down right now?"

"Mam, did you just call me Mam?! Am I getting the Mr. Big Official Trooper treatment right now? I don't think I appreciate that or your tone."

"Oh for Pete's sake, Lacey.give me a break. You are throwing some kind of breaking news at me in the middle of a really big and dangerous deal and we have Gladys now under the Volvo doing Lord knows what."

I looked and sure enough. There she was, under the Volvo. Looked like she was lying still and hopefully just listening but I guess with her I couldn't be absolutely sure. "Ok, I am sorry Luke. You are right. I meant to tell you before but I didn't think it meant anything and still not completely sure it does and it is a long story that we don't have time for right now. I will fill you in later ok?"

All I heard him say was, "damn it, Charlie is starting to move", then he hung up on me. I looked out the window and saw Gladys starting to move too. She was sliding out and scooting behind snow banks for cover and heading this way. I looked towards Charlie's and saw his door was open again. He had what looked to be a young girl covered in a blanket and he was pulling her to his truck. He was roughly jerking her along and then violently shoved her in the driver's side door, continuing to shove her over as he climbed in. His face was beet red and he looked livid. I couldn't hear him but he had to be yelling. I could see spit flying out of his mouth. I assumed he was cussing out the girl and everyone else in the world at that moment. It looked like he was having trouble getting his truck started by the way he was beating on the steering wheel. It finally must have turned over because I heard a bang and a cloud of black smoke floated up from the back end of it. Charlie slammed it into reverse and flew out of his driveway. It looked like he was going to head this way!

I ran downstairs and got to the door just as Gladys was opening it screaming "we can't let him get away! The black car is coming back this way from the other direction!"

I ran after her. No idea what we could do to stop either Charlie or Eddie. I am sure Luke and all the other law enforcement scattered about saw them and were giving chase as well. I couldn't see any of them but they had to be out there somewhere. Hopefully closer to this side of the lake than the other. Gladys was scrambling through the snow towards Earl's workshop. It was closer to the road than any of the houses. Other than getting a good look at them as they hopefully drove by, I had no idea what she was thinking. I'd no sooner caught up with her and the black Rover pulled into the Cook's driveway which is directly next door to Gladys' place. The Rover went right up and over the huge snow bank blocking the driveway, reversed back out and then backed into the driveway with the nose of the huge vehicle sticking out like it was ready for a quick getaway. It just sat there. Waiting.

We could hear Charlie's truck before we could see it. When we finally did see it, Charlie was hanging out the window screaming "you bitches. It was you that ruined my chances at a threesome. I oughta kill you." Charlie stopped his truck in front of LuAnn's driveway. He climbed out and I could see the anger in his eyes and spittal on his chin. He reached back into the truck and brought out a gun. I body slammed Gladys into a snow-bank and moved to lay down beside her. I heard Charlie's shot hit the door of Earl's shed and the door sprang open.

Gladys popped up screaming at Charlie "you dang fool you busted the damn door. That is the second door of mine you have busted this week! I'm gonna take that right out of your hide, you no good scoundrel!"

Charlie started to aim again but then I heard Eddie shouting to him. "You can kill them later. Hurry up and bring that bitch over here and make the swap so I can get out of here. All of your wildass shooting is going to attract attention."

I turned to look at Eddie. At least he had gotten Charlie to stop shooting at us for the moment and he wasn't trying to kill us. And it didn't seem like he knew that there were several cops nearby. At least I was praying they were close. I looked over to check on Gladys. No Gladys. WTF, where did she go? I tried to peek around without sticking my head too far up. Charlie had yanked the girl out of his truck and was walking past Gladys' house over to the Rover parked next door. He was focused on Eddie. Maybe he didn't trust him. Maybe he wasn't quite as dumb as he looked.

Gladys slipped back in beside me with a small smile on her face. I didn't dare talk to her cause I didn't want anyone looking our way. We stared in horror as Eddie took a small Asian girl out of the Rover and gave her hand to Charlie and Charlie shoved the small girl over to Eddie. Just as Eddie was going to put the girl into his Rover, Gladys jumped up screaming "Freeze Suckers!"

Everyone froze for a millisecond and then Eddie slowly turned to look at us, He burst out laughing. Gladys growled and let loose. Her first shot hit the Rover on the hood. It sounded like a cannon to me. I was nice and up close but had no idea what she was packing in the fanny pack that had been opened up while we were waiting.

Eddie had stopped laughing and everyone was still for a second more then all hell broke loose. Eddie tried to take a step back and brace himself but was a bit off balance with all the snow. He fired some shots in our direction but they went wide. I tried to push Gladys down and to get her inside the shed but she turned and fired back towards Charlie's truck. It looked like her aim was off again and that it was going to hit the back end. Her shot connected with the rag sticking out of the gas tank and the extra stick of dynamite she had stuck in there when she went missing. The truck exploded and flew up in the air crashing down and coming to rest upside down in the middle of the road. Charlie started going berserk and Eddie and his gang were scrambling to try and get back into the Rover. They didn't make much progress. Luke and all of his troops were flooding the area. They had Charlie, Eddie and everyone in handcuffs before my ears quit ringing.

Gladys was calmly putting her gun back into her fanny pack. I grabbed her and hugged her. "Gladys are you crazy? You almost got us killed! But I do love how you took care of Charlie's truck!"

"Well, okay, sure, maybe Eddie could have hit us but the odds were pretty low and I knew Charlie never would. He is a terrible shot. All things considered I think I did pretty ok. Maybe they could use me on the force. Make me a trooper here to protect the citizens around the lake."

Luke had walked up and laughed out loud and hugged Gladys. "You can be my assistant anytime Gladys. Though I am going to need you to turn over that fanny pack and I need you to tell me about all the firearms you have stashed out in the shed. I will take care of the fire power. You can be my eyes and ears on the ground."

Gladys smiled at him and turned to stick her tongue out at me. "See Miss Smarty-pants. Someone appreciates me."

CHAPTER 24

LUKE PULLED ME ASIDE AND GAVE
me a hug. I wanted to melt and just stay there
forever. He pulled back and looked into my
eyes before I could hide rising tears. "Hey babe, are you
ok? Did you get hurt by any of this?" He started checking me over.

"No, no, I am fine. Really, I'm fine. Just another
adrenaline-filled day."

He pulled me into his embrace again, "I'm worried
about you. It is all going to be ok, you know. Didn't I tell
you to trust me? Things have a way of working out. They
always do." He gave me an extra squeeze and then broke
away. "I've got to go wrap this up and get these girls to a
safe house while we find their families. It might take me
a while but I'll be back as quickly as I can. I still need to
hear the long story about Dexter and how he ties to Eddie
you know."

"Oh right, sure. Definitely. Gladys and I will be fine
here. We will see you when you get back." Luke gave me
a skeptical look and gave me strict orders to stay inside

and absolutely no guns. Geesh like I didn't know that already.

Gladys was still pumped from all the action this afternoon so getting her to sit still and chill was impossible. She kept asking me if I saw this or that. Quite excited about the adventure of the day. Which reminded me, I did see her action with the Volvo. "Gladys, what were you doing when you crawled under the Volvo earlier? I wonder why they never showed up when Charlie was making his exchange? What did they come along for I wonder?"

"Well, let me tell you what I heard. I snuggled up under there and they had no idea. It sounded like they were there only as back up if really needed and that they were supposed to pick up Dexter when the drop was done and take him to talk to Eddie someplace near here because Dexter had to be back in Grand Rapids later tonight and couldn't get to Mount Pleasant to Eddie's place. Guess that didn't end up mattering cause Eddie's not going to get to his place tonight either."

But I wonder why they didn't high tail it here when they heard Charlie shoot at us the first time? Seems like they would have figured that was an emergency."

"Maybe they couldn't for some reason. They possibly had car trouble or something."

"Gladys, what did you do?"

"I might have accidentally let all the air out of all their back tires and I was able to reach up under the car and grab some wires that came loose and fell off. Well after I used these handy wire cutters on them. I honestly don't know what all those were."

"You are amazing. Simply amazing. Let's clean up this white board mess and get a bite to eat. I can't figure out how Dexter and Gary are mixed up with Eddie but I am sure once I get back to Grand Rapids, Hunter and his team will help sort it all out."

We hadn't heard the front door opening or see Dexter standing there until we turned to head to the kitchen. We both jumped and screamed. I tried to sound calm as I asked him what he was doing here. It came out more shaky than I thought.

"Very good Lacey. Nice try. Too bad you aren't going to make it back to GR to work with Hunter to sort it all out. I think the tag line will read 'Cops miss capturing all of the notorious gang and young jilted murderer and nosy old lady murdered on New Year's Eve'. How sad."

"Nosy old lady? Watch it, you whippersnapper. And Lacey wasn't jilted. She was the jiltee."

"Damn, really?? I lost the office pool then. My money was on Chad dumping her. Though I knew of course that she didn't really kill him. But I couldn't exactly pick myself in the office pool could I? I joined the majority and put my money on you Lacey. Most everyone did, few picked Sara thinking she did it in a jealous rage over you."

"Me? What are you talking about? Sara wasn't jealous of me."

"Just so happens I know she was crazy about you. Not Chad so much. She confided in me at the Christmas party after she had had a few too many. I was new enough to the firm that she assumed I would be a sympathetic ear. Just fortuitous when I saw her bleeding out on Chad's office floor and that I caught him before he could call 911. He thought he could push me aside and have all of Eddie's business for himself and wasn't even going to bring me on as a partner in his new law firm. I showed him who was better suited to handle Eddie's account. Now let's quit blabbing and get on with this."

With that, Gladys fainted. I bent to help her and she winked at me. Dexter was fuming. "Good grief, move out of the way so I can get a clear shot at her. I'll put her out of her misery. I don't think my bullets can make it through both of you and do the job."

"That's enough Dexter! At least let me put her up on the couch and you owe it to me to fill in some blanks before you do me in." I had to keep him talking as long as I could. Not sure why but maybe I could think of some way to stop him. As I got Gladys on the couch she showed me the dainty pearl handled Derringer she had slipped out of her fanny pack. She hid it out of sight and I stood up blocking her as best I could. "So explain to me what is Gary's role in all this?"

"Gary? He is an idiot. He was going to go to Chad and tell him to stop the nonsense with Eddie. Chad had told both Gary and I about it but Gary wanted nothing to do with it. He was desperate for money but not enough to look past his holier than thou morals."

"How was it his fingerprints were on Chad's EH file and not yours?"

"I was smart and wore gloves. Duh. I took the contents and left the file. After I got back to my desk, I saw Gary head down to Chad's office. He stupidly picked the file up even though it was clear it was empty. Just another piece of evidence that I am the superior counselor."

"How did you get past the security cameras by the elevators and in the hall?"

Chad seemed exasperated but explained. "Very easy actually. There were two stairways up to the 8th floor nimrod. One for all of us grunts to do the bidding and the one close to Chad's office for all the supposedly premier lawyers to use."

I was running out of ideas on questions to ask. I didn't know how much time had passed and no idea where Luke was or when he would get back. I thought I felt Gladys shift and afraid Dexter would notice. "Oh, I know. What about Cindy? Weren't you afraid she would see you and catch you in the act?"

"No. I saw her come back to her desk so I knew she was done with Chad for the night and besides even if she caught me, she would have been fine with it. She didn't really like Chad just needed him to move up faster. She's pretty hot. I think I am going to bring her over to my firm to work on Eddie's account. Now move so I can get done and get out of here. Hey, aren't there blinds on these windows? Maybe you should close them so no one will see anything."

"How about we move to the kitchen? It would be easier to clean up. I sort of hate to ruin the carpet and everything. House rules are to clean up and leave it as you found it but if I am going to be dead my sister will probably give me a break on that. Just would like to make it easier for whoever finds us. Whenever they find us." I started to cry and then sob. Which just seemed to irritate Dexter.

"Oh for crying it out loud. You have got to be kidding. Are you really worried about the carpet? Do you honestly think any of this cartel gang would give a shit about your fucking carpet?"

I paused my sobbing, "ok, good point but how are you going to blame it on the guys in the Volvo? Where are they? What did you do with them?"

Dexter just glared at me for a second. "I didn't do anything with those idiots. They couldn't get their car started and the cops arrested them before Eddie was even taken in. Again my superior intellect prevails and I have thought of everything. I snagged a couple items with DNA from a couple of the other thugs when I was in Mount Pleasant the other day. I'll just leave those here to make it easier for the cops to figure out who did you in. Now I mean it. Move."

Gladys turned on her side and fired her gun. Not nearly as loud as the one she had used earlier but it seemed to be effective. She hit him in the hand that was holding the gun. Dexter dropped it, swearing like a sailor.

I tried scrambling to get the gun but I reached it just as Dexter laid his hand on it. I tried wrestling him but even wounded, he was strong. I heard Gladys let out a war hoop and she came flying on top of his back like a mad cat. It stunned him but didn't slow him down much. I never heard the door open but I heard Luke yell, "Freeze!"

We all looked up at him and Gladys slipped off of Dexter's back exclaiming, "it is about time you got back here! I was afraid he was going to shoot Lacey to shut her up long ago. That girl can carry on and on." Gladys glanced at me. "Well, I'm just sayin'....". She trailed off and at least had the decency to blush a little.

Luke tried not to smile while he put Dexter in cuffs and read him his rights, arresting him for the murder of Chad Wexler. Dexter was smart enough not to say a word as Luke pushed him out the door to one of the other officers that was standing on the porch.

"How did you know to get back up? What is going on?" I was very confused. Very thankful but confused.

Luke sighed and pulled both Gladys and I into a hug. "What am I going to do with you two?"

LuAnn started screaming through the intercom, "Lacey, you were giving me a heart attack. You owe me big time sister."

Luke explained. "I had turned the security system back on and fortunately LuAnn had just gone into her control room to call you when she saw Dexter come in the front door that the two of you had forgotten to lock when you came in. She immediately called me and started recording video and sound of what was going on here. I had just dropped the girls off at the safe house in Big Rapids and was headed back so I wasn't too far away. LuAnn patched me in so I could listen to what was going on and I was able to get back here as well. We got here just in time."

Gladys hugged him again, "I am so glad you did. I thought we were gonna be gonners."

Luke looked down at her and asked how she ended up having a gun when he had told her to give them all to him. She looked up at him defiantly "you didn't expect me to give you Pearl did you? Earl gave her to me and taught me how to shoot when we were first married. He said never could tell when I might need to protect myself. Guess he was right about that."

Murray showed up and asked if he could escort Gladys home. Luke said, "that is a good idea. I think we have all had enough excitement for one day." Murray took Gladys' hand and led her home and Luke stepped in the control room saying, "Goodnight LuAnn, I'll have someone get the tapes from you tomorrow" then he shut off the system.

Luke came back to me. Locked the front door and said, "Happy New Year Lacey Wheeler, I think it is going to be a great one.

EPILOGUE

NEARLY SIX WEEKS LATER AND just feeling like I could take a breather. Right after Luke and I rang in the New Year together celebrating my freedom, he followed me as I drove my trustworthy 4Runner Hank back to the city. I was interrogated multiple times but cleared of all charges. Derrick was still in jail waiting for his trial. The judge determined he was a flight risk and refused to set any bond. I heard through the grapevine that Derrick was furious and conniving with lawyers out of Chicago to get all the charges against him dropped. Which is really hard to imagine since they have him on tape confessing to multiple crimes.

Gladys and Murray were seeing more and more of each other. Murray was planning a spring trip to London and Paris for them. I think he would like to pop the question but Gladys is adamant about keeping her place and just being Murray's girl. Maybe she will think differently after Paris. I can't wait to hear her stories about how she is taking London and Paris by storm.

LuAnn had put me up for a couple weeks while we searched for a new place for me. I lucked out and got a small house in the country in Caledonia township. They have a two-acre minimum requirement so I didn't have any other houses right on top of me and it felt like my own little piece of heaven. I am still plugging away at FGE and my new house isn't too far of a commute. It's a little farther to Luke's place; he still has an apartment downtown. We're taking it slow on committing to actually living together. Not that I miss Chad but it feels too soon to make it more permanent. We stay at one place or the other together frequently. Although, now that I am thinking of Luke it has been a few days since I saw him. He was at some special training in Lansing for the big presidential debates coming to town in a couple months.

I am very excited because we are actually having a real, formal date for Valentine's Day. Luke's keeping all the details a surprise. I honestly don't care if we just grab JT's pizza and curl up together at home. Every time Luke looks in my eyes, he makes me feel so special. I cannot believe how lucky I am to have stumbled into meeting him. I can't wait for our date and seeing how our relationship grows.

Thinking back, I can't help but remember that all I wanted for Christmas was an alibi. But now, every time I look into Luke's eyes, I shudder at my good fortune. I didn't just get an alibi … I got the love of my life.

Linda Shoaf

About the Author

Linda Shoaf is an aspiring author born in California while her father was a medic in the Air Force. She relocated when he returned to Michigan to tackle the family farm. Her mother was a reading specialist and inspired Linda's love of reading and desire to write. *All I want for Christmas is an Alibi*, is Linda's first cozy mystery.

When she's not reading, writing, or thinking about new book ideas, Linda loves spending time with her family, watching and feeding birds, antiquing and a little bit of light gardening.

www.ingramcontent.com/pod-product-compliance
Lightning Source LLC
Chambersburg PA
CBHW032036240626
47154CB00003B/944